MALEVOLENT

THE PARANORMAL INVESTIGATOR #8

CHRISTOPHER CARROLLI

ISBN: 978-1-68046-752-9

Melange Books, LLC
White Bear Lake, MN 55110
www.melange-books.com

Published in the United States of America.

Cover Design by Caroline Andrus

As always, for my mother and Tara, and this time, I would also like to dedicate this book to someone who encouraged my writing every step of the way and who hoped to one day read my books, my pal, Ulysses "Mickey" Johnson (1949-2006). Thanks, Mick, always.

I would also like to take this space to extend one final thanks to Editor/Author Mel Duvall, who passed away in 2018. Mel edited "Black Mirror: The Paranormal Investigator—Book Six" and did an incredible job. She taught me so much about editing in such a short time. Thanks again, Mel, for everything. RIP.

FOREWORD

Hello Friends and Readers. Thank you for joining me on the paranormal investigators' eighth adventure. This one is sure to be another whirlwind ride, so fasten your seatbelts! But first, there are a few things I would like to mention before you begin reading *Malevolent*. People have asked me consistently whether or not they should read my books in the order of sequence. I rarely know how to answer this question. I know that as a reader myself, I like to read a series in order from the first book, but that's my personal preference. Several of my readers have told me that they've read my books in the backwards order. All of them have enjoyed doing so. They tell me that while they may know an event happened beforehand, they couldn't wait to read *how* it happened. So, if you are now reading my series for the first time, please by all means, continue. This brings me to my point.

In *Black Mirror*, I laid the foundation for a storyline that later flourished in *Shadows Among Us*, and has now reached its climax in *Malevolent*. That is the story of Susan's former patient, Dean Collier. *Malevolent* is a direct sequel to *Shadows Among Us*, even though that story has ended, and now a new one begins. Several events that occurred in the last book carry over into this book, but no need to worry. I quickly recap the events in the last book to make the new reader not feel lost, and to refresh the memories of those of you who have already read *Shadows Among Us*. An example is a scene in the first chapter. I have rewritten a scene from *Shadows Among Us*, this time, from the spirit's point of view. I have done this so the new reader may understand what happened to Lydia Collier, as her story continues in *Malevolent*.

A new storyline is emerging for Dylan, one that began in *Phantom in the Sky*, but again, that event is quickly recapped so that all readers can connect and relate, whether you've read that book yet or not. Keep your eyes on Tahoe, as a new storyline is setting the stage for him as well. But what is also crucial is not giving away spoilers from past books. That is the tricky part of writing a series, but hopefully, I have avoided this problem and left just enough mystery to leave the reader wondering. While past events are always important to my investigators, the here and now is the most important issue to the reader, and I have kept this in mind throughout.

So, new readers, old readers, thank you all and welcome aboard for another twisted whirlwind! Kick back, relax, but be mindful of any strange mists that suddenly surround you.

With Love,
    Chris

Christopher Carrolli
    December 17, 2018
    9:19 pm EST

Definitions

Clairaudience—

The Power or faculty of hearing something not present to the ear but regarded as having objective reality.

Doppelganger—

A ghostly double or counterpart of a living person. A German word meaning "double walker," a Doppelganger is said to be an omen of bad luck or impending death.

Malevolent—

1) Having, showing, or arising from intense, often vicious ill will, spite, or hatred.

2) Productive of harm or evil.

Skinwalker—

In Native-American culture, the skinwalker is thought to be a type of witch who has the ability to turn into, possess, or disguise themselves as an animal.

The Third Eye—

The third eye (also called the mind's eye or the inner eye) is a mystical and esoteric concept referring to a speculative invisible eye which provides perception beyond ordinary sight. Third eye is the extension of what the mind knowingly perceives. It is the subconscious awareness of the surroundings and interactions of the environment.

* Definitions on this page and throughout this book are provided by both Merriam Webster and Wikipedia.

1

AWAKENED

HIGH ABOVE THE GROUND, THE SPIRIT HOVERED LIKE A dark cloud. Disembodied and detached from the world it had once been a part of, the spirit continued to linger within it as a separate, unseen presence. Conscious thought was fleeting. Bits of random information presented themselves like abstract puzzle pieces. Some things the spirit recognized; some things it did not. Cohesive thought became temporary. As the bits of information strung together to form a meaning, suddenly the string of thought became broken by any number of interruptions: voices, faces, sounds, past memories. Bound by the chains of death, the spirit lacked a physical host to bring it to full, thriving life.

Like the countless beings whose heads it hovered high above, it had once existed as they had in the hustle and bustle of what it once knew as life. A single memory recurred over and over, each time bringing the spirit closer to a knowledge it faintly understood. Some time ago, an explosion had ripped through its once human and conscious mind, forever shattering memories and the knowledge it collected throughout its existence. A sulfuric taste, a tinge of gunpowder lingered on its ghostly pallet forever.

The memory kept showing a hand raising a pistol, a finger pulling a trigger, and then the spirit saw the explosion again.

Fire, blood, and then life faded to black.

Then, the world had come back into view. The spirit's new existence had hovered above the ground, bodiless, lost, and unaware. It recognized emotions it once knew: regret, confusion, and unending pain. Yet its attention to such things soon evaporated, erased by the happenings of a world that continued on without it. Then the suicide memory would play out again, through the boundless hell of repetition.

After its violent release from the world, the spirit recognized the faces of loved ones left behind. Tears streaming down their faces, they'd called out the given name the spirit once adhered to in this world.

"Dean, Dean, Dean."

But memories of Dean's existence played out in random images: Mother, walking him to school every day; Father, pitching him practice softballs in the yard. Lauren, walking down the aisle in her wedding dress, and Lydia, taking her first steps and clasping onto his legs—her first finish line. The spirit felt a connection to all of them, but none so like Lydia. Lydia: blood of its blood, flesh of its flesh. Lydia, its one mark, its single legacy left in this world.

The spirit of Dean Collier watched Lydia grow into a smart, successful, and beautiful young woman. When Lydia married, the spirit felt a strange sense of contentment, as if its job had been done, as if it could rest—at least for the time being. Rest it had, though rest was sporadic. The images of its own human demise continued, yet the spirit became accustomed to the knowledge that the images would consume its existence forever. It knew what it had done.

The spirit continued to linger in the strangest form of respite until dark, shadowy figures awakened its existence. Unlike humans, the shadows were not constrained to the ground beneath them. The shadows took to the air, as well as the ground. They corralled the spirit's floating form and danced around it in a flurry.

The shadows had dragged the spirit down to the earthly floor and forced it to accompany them on a frightening whirlwind.

Through it all, the familiar shadows seemed to be sending messages the spirit could not understand. The spirit saw its earthly name written in blood. Four bloody letters dripped down a wooden door. It saw a woman's face, a blonde woman it knew but couldn't pinpoint. Her identity was an answer that existed within its memory, but her name was a word that failed to form on ghostly lips, a name that drifted away in a sea of past memories.

A shadow whispered to its consciousness.

"Susan."

Susan.

A wave of shadowy hands produced glimpses of the past. In life, the spirit once sat across from Susan. She had worn a white coat, the keeper of Dean's innermost thoughts and feelings. The spirit remembered Susan trying to help. She believed in Dean. The spirit recalled feelings of gratitude toward her but with a hidden sense of skepticism. It remembered a dormant thought from long ago, one that questioned why Susan believed in him when others had not.

The shadows incited the spirit to remember, and remember it had. It remembered the shadows. They had haunted its life. They watched when its earthly hand pulled the trigger. Now, they had awakened it, stirring its dormant anger into a seething, malevolent wrath.

Susan.

Dean had warned Susan about the shadows. She failed to listen. Now, the shadows sought to contain Dean's spirit as a prisoner. The spirit would not let that happen. Fear was no longer a factor; life had already ended.

The spirit had mustered all of its preternatural energy and lunged at the shadows, but the shadows were quick, lashing back like a collective crack from a ringmaster's whip. The spirit felt itself aiming, and then striking out like a cobra, but the dark dancing forms remained impervious to its presence. The shadows were the masters. They would shape its boundless soul into the malevolent force they had conjured.

The shadows became as relentless as time was unending. The spirit saw Lydia's face and the slight trace of its own earthly existence in her green eyes and rich red hair. The shadows were warning the spirit, invoking its closest earthly connection as a hostage. The spirit failed to fully comprehend. It would follow the shadows. It would adhere to them and watch helplessly in an agonizing effort to understand.

Evoking a powerful energy, the shadows attracted the spirit like a magnet and dragged it through a misty, clouded whirlwind. As wisps of thin mist evaporated, the image of a white stately mansion became clearer and more solid. Large white columns upheld vast terraces above. Below, stone walkways spiraled through flower gardens leading to the front entrance. At the front door, Susan and two others stood waiting to enter the house.

The spirit knew the house, by instinct as well as by sight. It had seen it before in some small space of time, but time seemed to be an everlasting duration where the past and the present coexisted together. Lydia, this was Lydia's house. The spirit, unseen, watched as the connection between Lydia and Susan was revealed.

On the tennis court, Lydia shook Susan's hand. The spirit listened to their words.

"...a friend of my father. Is that true?"

Lydia mentioned her father. The spirit remembered being her father.

"A friend in one way. I was his psychiatrist," Susan replied.

Psychiatrist. The spirit knew the word. Suddenly, a past memory played out alongside the present. Susan sat across from him—him—Dean. She'd clasped his hands in hers.

"You can overcome this, Dean," she said. "You can put your life back together."

Abruptly, the memory vanished. The present had moved slightly forward.

The spirit watched as Lydia, Susan, and her friends adjourned to the small study. Lydia spoke of how her father had ultimately been a good man. The spirit heard something in her voice: yearning, constant grief, overwhelming love. A fleeting notion of heartbreak consumed the spirit. Then, the feeling faded as Susan's words diverted its attention.

"I saw the good in Dean, but I'm afraid I failed to fully recognize his illness because I believed in him...I wish I could have saved him."

Saved him. There would have been no saving him from the shadows. There would be no absolution for his self-murder. The spirit remained damned to its own repetitive hell, where the shadows could now haunt it throughout eternity. Waking the spirit from its only perception of rest, the shadows had forced it to behold the world in its current state and listen to the words of its heartbroken offspring.

"Something had been turning my Dad into a different man. During those fights with my Mom, something would change him. He would turn almost —malevolent."

The word reverberated through the spirit's consciousness —malevolent.

Susan was a liar. The spirit sensed it, recognizing some secret, secondary agenda. Her main concern was not the life the spirit had once been. The spirit recognized feelings of guilt emanating from Susan, but there was something more, something it failed to understand.

The spirit noticed Susan's friend, the young woman with long blonde hair. A strange glow radiated from her forehead, just between her eyes. The spirit moved within the slight shimmering, trying to attract the young woman's attention which remained fixed on Lydia. The spirit could make its presence known, but the young woman sat rapt in Lydia's words. A plump young man sat alongside her, listening with ears that heard beyond the sounds of the physical world. Susan's friends were able to communicate with the world beyond, a fact the spirit knew automatically.

"Well, during one of our sessions, he kept referring to 'shadows.'"

Susan spoke again. She knew about the shadows. Now, she believed. The spirit watched as Lydia handed Susan an object. It recognized the object, but it failed to grasp the word. The everyday item from the stream of life now lingered in the passage of eternity as a vaguely remembered memento. A fleeting word caught the spirit's attention—*video*.

A flash of memory: moving pictures, video, watching Lydia dance through the camera lens, Lauren shielding her face from the camera, Mom and Dad glancing at each other, then at the camera, bashfully scrambling for words. The spirit saw its life, its body, its face. It remembered speaking to the camera. It remembered watching those precious moments over and over.

The present moment sped fast into the future. Lydia bid Susan and the others goodbye at the doorstep. A sensation swept the spirit, a strong energy, a feeling of mistrust. Susan was the cause of the suspicion. The shadows had revealed it.

The spirit knew how to muster its energy and then direct it toward a physical source. It focused on the feelings it now felt about Susan. It projected the inkling of distrust onto Lydia. She would sense its energy, its message. Blood of its blood, flesh of its flesh.

Wrinkles of doubt formed on Lydia's face. Her green eyes narrowed in wonder. Back in her small study, Lydia searched on her computer until she found words and pictures of Susan. The spirit's projection had worked. Lydia received its message, its warning—Susan had an ulterior motive.

Hovering above Lydia's head, the spirit witnessed her disappointment, confusion, and frustration. Susan had not been completely forthcoming. Now, Lydia knew what the spirit had sensed about Susan. It watched as Lydia rose from her desk chair and walked to the living room's wooden staircase.

Suddenly, the room darkened as if a thousand shadows eclipsed all visible light. The house was plunged into a darkness Lydia could not see. The spirit felt their presences. It heard the strange popping, plucking noises they made. The shadows had returned.

They'd come back for the spirit. They would force it to accompany them on another whirlwind, or so it assumed.

A shadow shot past Lydia at the top of the stairs. Light flickered intermittently through the shadowy darkness as the spirit soared up the stairs. Lydia teetered backwards. The spirit emitted its energy toward Lydia and projected it around her, attempting to create an invisible bond. Lydia clasped the railing and balanced herself on the staircase. Undeterred, she reached the top step and walked into the family room. The spirit followed.

Lydia screamed as another shadow jumped out in front of her. Then, the shadows multiplied, baring blazing red eyes as they invoked her fear. They chased her, edging her into a fit of hysteria before she ran out onto the balcony. The spirit struggled to intervene, mustering its energy, but projecting nothing more than a sudden wind that swept the room unnoticed. Cornered by the shadows, Lydia backed up against the balcony railing. The spirit watched helplessly as Lydia lost her balance and tumbled backwards over the edge.

From above, it saw Lydia's broken body strewn on the stone platform below. Myriad emotions besieged the spirit. It felt the sudden rape of pain, defeat, and loss, but worst of all—rage. The spirit raged against the shadows, a futile attempt to affect their dark, ghostly presences. The shadows simply watched, goading the spirit's anger and fury, taunting it with their untouchable superiority. Then, the shadows vanished. The eclipsing darkness withdrew and departed.

The spirit hovered above Lydia's body, watching as energy rose from her. Lydia's soul lifted high above, where the restless spirit could not reach it. Gone was the spirit's only physical connection to this world. The spirit once known as Dean lingered invisibly, unacknowledged, and darkly remembered.

Rage consumed it. Sudden evil overwhelmed the one hint of love it had clearly understood. A feeling of malevolence besieged the spirit. It would avenge. The shadows did this. Susan had brought them here. It would make her pay. It would consume her with its ghostly venom. It would steal her body long enough to fully awaken and understand. She would be its host. Then, it would destroy her.

The spirit projected its wrath. Windows shattered. Curtains wafted. Doors slammed. It would perfect the force it now wielded with a gathering strength. What had once lingered as a simple, benign energy now strengthened into something more, something malignant, something malevolent.

THE SHADOWS THEN BROUGHT THE SPIRIT TO AN abandoned cemetery it recognized, where fallen angels made of stone reignited a fear it once knew. In this moment, the past and present came together. It watched Susan walk through the cemetery, snapping pictures of the wayward stone faces depicting judgment and sorrow. She had caused Lydia's death, and now she sauntered through this cursed garden searching for answers, oblivious to the fatal consequences of her actions.

The spirit recognized Susan's friends. The young man who heard the sounds the shadows made. Battlefield reverberations once ravaged this hallowed ground and now echoed throughout the spirit world. This young man heard all of it. He walked alongside the young blonde woman who gazed with a glimmering psychic eye unseen on her forehead. They strolled together, searching for answers from the spirit world. Could the spirit attract their attentions? Could it inflict its wrath upon Susan right here, right now?

Here, the outdoors offered no windows to shatter, and the spirit's energy was not strong enough to crack the stone cold statues. Mustering its energy to produce a forceful wind would have no effect. Sound, the spirit felt the urge to create sound. Perhaps the young man would hear it. Perhaps the girl's third eye would catch a fleeting glimpse of its rage.

Magnifying its own strength was an everlasting and ongoing

endeavor. As time passed, the spirit grew stronger, strong enough to affect physical matter, yet its strength remained confined. Whether that was a result of the shadows' enslavement or its own limitation remained a mystery, but it would continue to focus and project, until its wrath was heard.

The spirit plunged itself deep down to the core of its once human existence. It remembered the sound of its human voice. Gathering all of its strength, all of the energy that it was, the spirit focused to produce sound. A mournful agonizing groan erupted from it, one that would fall upon deaf, earthly ears. The spirit struggled with the sound of her name, until it projected a low, guttural moan that called to her.

"*SU—SAN...*"

The spirit heard its own distorted voice, slower, devoid of emotion, the opposite of life—death. The sound echoed, yet Susan hadn't flinched. She kept clicking away with the camera. The plump young man walked, enrapt by the sounds of the past. He failed to hear the spirit's voice, its single attempt to be heard. The spirit seethed, angered to be unacknowledged and confined to the realm of the dead, an identical world unseen from the earth.

The shadows, alerted by the sound of the spirit's voice, surrounded it once again. They blocked its view and obstructed its path with their darkness. Then, the spirit saw the world in a flurry of passing images as the shadows whisked it away once again.

———

THE WRATHFUL SPIRIT BECAME LOST IN THE ESSENCE OF time. Again, time moved slightly forward, yet all moments merged together as one. The spirit had awakened again, overwhelmed by a single knowledge that penetrated its limited understanding; the shadows had been vanquished. Never again would the spirit be summoned by the shadows and forced to be an unwilling witness to their destruction. The spirit could see by an abundance of untainted light that the terror inflicted by the shadows had ended.

Now, the spirit lingered in unfamiliar surroundings: winding, twisting roads, scenic views, and palatial houses. Two words proudly boasted from atop an arched iron gateway—*King's Haven*. Inexorably, the spirit was drawn once again like a magnet, this time toward an immense, copper-toned brick house. The spirit hovered above the house's long walkway, the lampposts, and higher above the gable windows. Then, the spirit's surroundings suddenly changed as it occupied the house's interior. Swiftly, it followed a stone catacomb structure all the way down from the ceiling to a hearth below. Soon, it became lost in the dim surroundings.

Then, Susan appeared out of nowhere. Instinctively, the spirit understood. The immediate surroundings belonged to Susan. The spirit remembered its wrathful agenda. It remembered channeling its energy to find Susan. Now, it had found its way into Susan's home.

It watched her every move as she pranced around the house, comfortable in her surroundings. After flicking a switch and flooding the room with light, she plopped on the couch and rotated both hands across the plush leather on each side of her. The spirit recognized not only Susan's contentment, but her great relief to finally be home.

The spirit hovered just above her head. It watched as she rose from the couch and examined every aspect of the room and every item in it, as if she were experiencing them for the first time. The spirit would possess her. It would steal her body. She would host its malevolent presence, but it would watch her first. The spirit sensed that something was not right about her.

As it neared her, it sensed a vast emptiness, an unexplainable void. The spirit often felt a certain low-grade heat, a spark around humans, the presence of something greater than the physical body. The feeling the spirit got from Susan was that of a cold empty shell, as if she had no soul, as if she were already dead. She was not like other humans.

Susan's attention was suddenly diverted. Something made her

shift her eyes toward the living room window. Quickly, she spun around and flicked the light switch off, drowning the room once again in darkness. She ran to the window and peeped outside. Bright light sliced through the curtains and spun through the dimness. When the light vanished, Susan was gone.

The spirit lingered in the dark, searching for the woman it had watched so closely. It sensed her presence, yet it failed to see her, as if she remained hidden. A beeping noise blared from the front door, followed by a loud click. The front door opened, and the same woman stepped back inside the house—Susan. She turned on the lights, waved from the front door, and closed it behind her.

Susan stepped through the entranceway and removed her jacket. She hadn't been wearing a jacket before. She hadn't even been wearing the same clothes. Something was altogether different about her. As she walked into the kitchen, the spirit noticed her slow, graceful steps differed greatly from the quick, clumsy plodding it witnessed only moments ago.

Something was not right about her. Something was different. The spirit remained lost, once again, in confusion.

2

THE OTHER SUSAN

To the unsuspecting eye, it would've seemed like Susan Logan's doppelganger had appeared out of nowhere. She had penetrated the thick brick walls of Susan's home, parting atoms and molecules, moving as if she walked through water. Angus Marlowe had taught her to utilize her ghostly form and slip through sturdy walls. She remembered well her mentor's lessons, which seemed like a lifetime ago. Now, she existed in this big vibrant world on her own, equally and freely commuting between her physical doppelganger self and her ghostly form. Her ghostly invasion allowed her to enter Susan's stately home unseen.

Her six month escapade of living life as Susan Logan had abruptly been quashed. For a while, she'd been able to master Susan's identity. After all, she shared Susan's thoughts. But Susan and her friends caught on to her. They'd traced her footsteps and excursions through the credit cards she'd stolen from Susan's wallet.

Yet she'd been able to obtain extra cards in Susan's name and other forms of credit. She not only knew Susan's social security number, but pin numbers, and important dates as well. She knew every aspect of Susan, inside and out. She *was* Susan, to some large extent. Still, she'd raised too much suspicion with her spending and frequent cash advances.

Susan moved fast, alerting her creditors that her identity had been stolen. Access to all forms of credit abruptly terminated. Her cash supply dwindled. Her escapade was over. As Susan's double, the world felt as if it had stopped turning. She'd been cornered with nowhere to turn, nowhere to go—except home.

Inside the empty house, she basked in the long awaited comfort, relieved that the first phase of her plan had been accomplished. She'd made it safely inside, knowing well that Susan had not yet arrived home. The rest of her plan was to reside here in Susan's home, in plain sight, yet distinctly unseen. In the day when Susan worked at the hospital, she would live comfortably in her physical semblance. Then, before Susan returned home, she would fade back into her ghostly form and linger until Susan left again in the morning.

It wouldn't be forever, she told herself; just until she could devise some other plan, one that would allow her to freely live out her physical existence. She thought of other options like running away and assuming another name, but that would be difficult. She would need to locate someone with the criminal expertise to supply her with a fake identity, social security number, driver's license, birth certificate, and more. It wasn't that it couldn't be accomplished, but it would take time, time she didn't have at the moment.

She'd also thought of another option, fading into her ghostly form and living out her existence like an unseen ghost, constantly being overwhelmed by Susan's thoughts, words, and feelings. That was not an option at all. She would never give her up her physical existence or the thriving world around her. She didn't have to, not as long Susan remained alive.

Light flooded the living room after she flicked a switch. The brightness provided a much needed relief to her eyes. She felt them widen after enduring hours of shadowy dimness. Yet the small celebration was short lived. Sudden emotions overwhelmed her. This time, the feeling of relief upon arriving home didn't belong to her.

Instinct drew her attention to the living room window. Quickly, she turned and flicked off the light switch. She moved silently in the darkness, and then stood staring out the window. The light from a pair of headlights barreled through the curtains. A car pulled into the driveway. A van followed closely behind it.

Susan was home.

Instantly, she faded into her ghostly form, hoping that Susan and whoever it was with her hadn't seen the living room light before she'd flicked it off. A mere ghost in the darkness, she felt the sudden sense of not being alone, as if someone lingered in the house with her, watching. She gazed through the gloom and noticed no one. Turning her attention back to the window, she watched as the van backed away. A figure neared the front door —Susan.

She watched as the mirror image of herself stepped into the house, turned on the lights, and waved to someone outside. She remained unflinching in her ghostly form. Susan would never see her unless she revealed herself to her, and that was not part of her plan. Like an invisible spy, an unseen invader, she examined Susan's every move. The late April chill had made Susan don a light jacket. The other Susan watched as she slung it over the sofa.

She noticed how the highly esteemed Susan Logan walked to her kitchen and poured herself a glass of wine from a bottle she took from the fridge. A wave of what felt like envy washed over her as she studied Susan. Here was the perfection of the original being, the master copy, a height she would never achieve. If she watched her long enough, she knew she could perfect every aspect, every facial expression, and every graceful movement Susan Logan performed naturally. She felt those aspects of Susan, but some things were hard to imitate. Not inhabiting a physical body on a permanent basis made her human form heavy and clumsy, yet she became more natural with practice and time.

Her graceless, heavy-footed lumbering was one reason Leah

Leeds exposed her when she'd attempted to fool the paranormal investigators six months ago. Not to mention Leah Leeds possessed a powerful third eye, one that Angus had warned her about. She had failed to infiltrate the paranormal team, but she would dwell in the dimness as long as she had to because to the outside world, she *was* Susan Logan.

She watched Susan sit down at the table and chug the glass of wine in front of her. The feeling of relief exuded from her, a feeling she shared automatically. But one matter remained unsolved to the real Susan, one that beleaguered her thoughts and invoked her sleepless nights. That was the ghostly form that stood unseen right in front of her; her exact double, watching from only feet away as Susan relaxed in the privacy of her spacious kitchen.

Suddenly, the strangest feeling swept over her. The sensation was sudden and abrupt like a light, unexpected breeze. She gazed around the room with ghostly eyes and saw nothing. Again, she felt the presence of another, as if while she watched Susan, something equally unseen watched her.

———

THE SPIRIT SENSED SOMETHING UNSEEN IN DARKNESS, something that remained when Susan reentered the house and turned on the lights again. Through its confusion, the spirit noticed an outline, a shape, but then it dashed away.

3

ARRIVING HOME

A WAVE OF RELIEF WASHED OVER HER AS SHE PULLED into her driveway. Susan glanced into the rearview mirror and noticed the other pair of headlights behind her. Sidney, having recently become staunchly overprotective, followed her home again, although there had been no need. Another case had been closed tonight. Another mystery would remain buried in the woods beyond the Taylor farm. Tonight, she and the team were not only relieved, but lucky, and thankful to have walked away unharmed.

"Are you sure you'll be okay?" Sidney asked when she walked to the van's driver's side.

"Yes, Sidney, I'll be fine."

"I'll wait and watch you enter the house."

"And then go straight home, Sidney. You're exhausted. We all are after tonight."

"I'll do that Dr. Logan, but not until I watch you go inside."

She gave him a crooked smile, one she often used to convey how ridiculous he was being, but she obliged him. After keying in the security code, she stepped through the door, turned on the lights, and waved to him from the doorstep. Everything was fine. She watched him back out of her driveway and leave.

It was good to be home. The terror of the past week had ended. She didn't care what kind of headache she had in the morning; she needed a glass of wine. She poured a glass from the bottle of Merlot she kept in fridge, and then sat at her kitchen table.

The shadows were gone, but a darker prospect continued to linger over her head like a storm cloud. Her doppelganger remained out there somewhere, unseen, invisible, except for when she showed herself. Then, she appeared to an unsuspecting world as Susan Logan. Susan and the team had been ready to find her elusive double, hoping to utilize Leah's third eye in a sort of psychic search. They'd been discussing such a possibility when Tahoe showed up at room 208, claiming to have been followed by menacing shadowy figures.

And followed he was. Afterwards, every member of the team experienced a unique, individual encounter with the shadows. The shadows had spread among them like a contagion. Susan remembered how a shadow chased her from the spot where she now sat, into the living room, where another shadow painted a name in blood on the inside of her front door. The bloody letters comprised the name of a former patient, one she'd failed long ago— Dean. While under her care, Dean Collier had lodged a .32 caliber bullet into his temple. She'd underestimated his mental illness, and then blamed the medication rather than his bi-polar disorder.

The shadows had resurrected the guilt she felt over Dean's suicide. Her failure could never be undone. She thought of Dean now. How he lunged at her in the dream she had the other night. The red mask of anger and rage on his face caused her heart to leap while she slept. Dean had never unleashed his rage upon her; in fact, she'd never witnessed it. But in the dream, his real and boundless fury erupted and targeted her. Then, she woke.

The search for her doppelganger was temporarily postponed. She and the team helped Tahoe battle the deadly shadows.

Afterward, they all sat around the picnic table on Brett's back patio, discussing the night's events, when the conversation turned to her mysterious double's whereabouts. She'd watched Tahoe close his eyes and envision. When he opened them again, he spoke to her.

"You will find her," he said. "Soon."

What did soon mean? Tonight, tomorrow, two weeks from now? Tahoe hadn't seen further, but he continued.

"I see your face and her face, identical eyes staring into each other's."

Now, Tahoe remained at the farmhouse. Brett invited him to stay a while longer, and Tahoe accepted. Tonight was Thursday. Gathering the team together tomorrow was impossible; not all of their schedules were free. So, they'd decided to take a day to let their minds clear of the events surrounding the past couple of days. On Saturday, they would meet again at Brett's house. Perhaps with Leah and Tahoe combining their clairvoyant minds, they'd be able to snake out her doppelganger and end this situation once and for all.

The relief she felt in this moment seemed only temporary. Sitting just behind that relief was the disturbing knowledge that tonight, the investigators experienced psychic warnings about her. The shadows had invoked visions even in Brett and Dylan, neither of whom was clairvoyant. Brett claimed to have envisioned the wolf chasing an unseen entity through her yard. Sidney's clairaudient ear had heard her crying out. Leah envisioned Susan pushing her down the stairs in this house, something Susan would never do. The warnings were minute glimpses, omens of an imminent future that plunged her into a state of fear.

Worse was the knowledge that the shadows had shown Susan a similar vision to what Leah had described. Susan saw her own face, forlorn, with bloodshot eyes casting a menacing stare. Susan was startled at the sight of herself in the vision, but equally disturbing was the question of whose face she saw, hers or her doppelganger's? The fear made her heart pound, her mind roam in a thousand directions, and her eyes dart from one end of the room to another.

Physician, heal thyself. How often she'd heard that phrase. Lately, she found herself less able to adhere to it. Being trapped in the blue realm six months ago affected her much more than she'd let on to the team. She was their leader. She didn't feel comfortable allowing them to experience her vulnerability, her weakness, the human flaw of fear that existed in her as much as it did any of her patients. The blue realm was a nightmare she never wanted to experience again. This was another reason she wanted to find her doppelganger as quickly as possible. She wanted it all to be over. She'd much rather return to chasing demons and ghosts in old haunted houses.

Susan tried to envision Tahoe's prediction, a face to face encounter with her doppelganger. Thousands of possible scenarios merged together in her mind. She couldn't even imagine how it would occur, but she was ready. Susan shuddered inside, realizing that her intent was to rid the world of this living thing, this being with her face and her body, once and for all.

A sudden draft swept by her. Slowly, Susan lowered her glass and looked around her. No windows remained open in the house. She looked over at the wall by the stove, where the first shadow had rolled down and then rose up in front of her. There were no shadows now. She sat alone in her kitchen. Maybe the draft had blown down through the chimney flue and into the hearth. Maybe it was just her mind. Physician, heal thyself. She got up from the table and poured herself another glass of wine.

———

SIDNEY ESCORTED SUSAN HOME AGAIN TONIGHT. THIS time, he allowed her to convince him to wait in the driveway until she waved from the door. He agreed, not wanting her to realize how frightened he was for her. Sidney remained quietly disturbed over the altercation he, Brett, and Dylan had with the shadows.

The shadows had invoked his deafness, causing Sidney to hear sounds he couldn't explain.

He'd stood in Freddy Nash's dining room, bewildered by the shadows and listening to the intermittent sounds they produced. He'd heard slamming doors and Susan crying out for help. Her desperate plea sounded different than when he'd first heard her, after she'd gone into the Black Mirror. Yet simultaneously, Susan sat waiting for them in room 208 along with Leah and Tahoe. The quick clairaudient interlude was a message from the shadows, one that became crystal clear. Sidney had heard the sounds of the future, bits and pieces of what was to come, audible snippets that comprised an ominous warning.

Sidney and the team concluded that Susan was in danger. Exchanging quick, stolen glances whenever Susan looked away, they remained convinced the looming peril would be brought about by her doppelganger. Sidney could think of no other reason for Susan's impending predicament.

Now, the team would remain vigilant concerning Susan. They would watch over her at all times. Tahoe's revelation of a face to face encounter hastened their plans to search for Susan's doppelganger. When he left Brett's farmhouse with Susan, the rest of the team was forming some sort of plan to do just that. Susan's doppelganger had walked out of the Black Mirror, stepped into the physical world, and disappeared somewhere within it. It was up to the team to undo this imbalance. After all, they were responsible for it.

Arriving home, Sidney gazed around his apartment. Only a few nights ago, the shadows filled his living room and even spread across the ceiling. The popping, plucking noises he heard had been theirs. The shadows taunted him with the past and warned him of the future. Now, he stood alone amid the stillness and the quiet. The shadows were gone, yet Sidney couldn't help but feel a new unseen danger lingering somewhere close by, waiting to happen.

THE IMAGE OF SUSAN PUSHING HER DOWN THE STAIRS would not leave her mind. Leah recalled the vision clearly, how the figure of Susan pushed her with powerful arms, how she felt herself falling backwards. She remembered the ghastly semblance in the vision, the forlorn, ragged face, and the menacing eyes that glared back at her. Something lingered behind those eyes— something malevolent. Leah wouldn't accept the psychic suggestion that the figure in the vision was Susan; it couldn't be. Surely, the Susan in the vision was Susan's doppelganger, a sinister agent hell bent on maintaining her existence at all costs.

Leah had experienced the vision standing at the top of her own staircase. The shadows showed her the vision, a mental image so real she nearly lost her balance. Instinctively, she'd known the vision depicted a future event. The vision came as a warning about Susan, an omen that more than just shadows awaited her and the team. That was only two nights ago, and it wasn't the first time Leah was visited by the shadows. The first time, they nearly burned her house down. She stared at the black hole in her white carpeting, a stark reminder that the shadows had been here.

She arrived home from Brett's farmhouse only minutes ago. After Sidney left with Susan, Tahoe reminded them of his vision of two Susan's. Then, they discussed the possibility of a psychic search for Susan's double.

"Our vision quest last night was a success," Leah pointed out. "There's no reason to think we won't be able to find Susan's double."

"That may be easier said than done, Little One," Tahoe replied. "Our search for the truth was guided by my great-grandfather. I believe he was largely responsible for helping us see into the past. I imagine that this would be different. We'd be gazing into the present world, searching for Susan's identical match, a being that may or may not be visible to our combined focus."

"But if you remember, our vision quest began in the present. It started out that way."

"True," Tahoe said. "But we must be diligent in our search,

rather than waiting for the answers to be shown to us. This time, we must look for them." Tahoe paused, narrowing his eyes in thought. "Doppelganger. I have heard the legends, but I continue to be amazed by the tale Brett has told me of recent events. Besides helping Susan, it is another reason I've decided to stay. This I must see with my own eyes."

"Doppelgangers have this sort of dual identity as both ghost and human," Brett said. "They're able to vanish into some ghostly form."

"That *is* part of the legend," Tahoe agreed.

"We watched Taryn do it," Leah said. "She moved through walls in her ghostly form."

At this, Tahoe raised his eyebrows, and then closed his eyes for a moment. Leah sensed that something about this revelation stirred a thought in Tahoe's mind.

"It appears that once the physical form is destroyed, so is the Doppelganger." Brett's conclusion made clear their impending strategy, to physically destroy Susan's doppelganger.

"But would she become a ghost?" Sidney argued. "Susan is still alive and according to Angus' black tome—"

"The ghostly form would perish also." Leah remembered her father's conclusions when deciphering the tome.

"Precisely," Tahoe said. "No human has two ghosts. If the Doppelganger dies while Susan lives, it is the end of her deadly double."

A silence ensued, one that told Leah it was time go home. The chaotic night had ended. Now, after showering, she relaxed in her living room in front of the TV. For just a brief moment, she hoped to find normalcy before she and Tahoe embarked on yet another vision quest.

———

DRIVING HOME, DYLAN COULD THINK OF NOTHING ELSE other than the visions the shadows had shown him and the images they planted in his mind. His memory of the night up on Eagle Rock Mountain stopped short with the flood of green light that had drowned him in its brightness. The next thing he remembered was trekking down the mountain and suddenly being aware of his surroundings. That's when he'd called Sidney to pick him up. Dylan assumed he'd spent the night up on the mountain, lost and confused from a drunken stupor. He couldn't have been more wrong. According to Sidney, Dylan had been missing for twenty-four hours.

He'd undergone a hypnosis session with Susan, a futile attempt to recall his forgotten memory of that evening. Subsequent attempts had also proven to be fruitless. After being enveloped in the phantom object's green light, blackness filled a void of time that seemed lost forever.

The shadows had changed all of that.

During his first encounter with the shadows, they caused him to live that moment up on Eagle Rock all over again. He saw it all, as if he were experiencing it a second time. After the flood of green light, Dylan saw bright, white, rectangular lights moving above him. He felt a cold, hard surface beneath him. For an instant, he'd felt like he was suffocating, then air filled his lungs. His memory of that night had proceeded a little further, all because of the shadows. They *knew* what happened to him.

Arriving home, Dylan punched in the security code for the front gate, and then parked the car in the four-car garage of his stately home. He strolled to the front door, thinking of his second encounter with the shadows. The Eagle Rock memory had flashed through his mind again. He'd stood transfixed, seeing nothing else but the events he'd buried deep within his mind, but on that second occasion, something was different. He remembered a hole being cut into the suffocating plastic mask over his mouth, allowing the air to surge into his lungs once again. The memory had progressed a little further, and then the scene in the vision changed.

He'd seen himself standing in the middle of a vast field,

watching as someone from a distance walked closer and closer toward him. It was a boy, a boy he'd never seen before. As the boy neared, Dylan noticed his red hoodie sweatshirt. The hood was draped over the boy's head, where dark bangs jutted out from underneath. Suddenly, the boy stopped walking and stood close enough for Dylan to see him. The boy stood and watched him. That's when Dylan saw the boy's eyes. Two big, black, opaque orbs stared back at him. Then, Dylan had felt Sidney shaking him out of the trance the shadows induced.

Who was the mysterious boy? How was he connected to Dylan's experience on Eagle Rock Mountain? The memory of that night had progressed a little further. Still, Dylan remained unable to place the boy in any of the minute fragments of memory he'd been able to recall. Not only was the boy unfamiliar, but so was the field.

Dylan had even entertained the notion of inciting the shadows to help him see more, but Susan, Tahoe, and the rest of the team admonished him for that idea, and how right they'd been. Tonight had ended in a mind-bending paranormal encounter that would become an unforgettable chapter in the society's history. He and the rest of the team had watched as the shadows sought to claim Tahoe's soul and lost. Yet gone with the shadows was the truth about what happened that night up on Eagle Rock. The shadows had tweaked his memory and left him wondering what happened afterwards.

He didn't want to think about it anymore, not tonight. A bitter resignation consumed him, one that convinced him that if he was meant to know, he would—someday. But now was not that time. He remembered the shadow that lifted its ghostly finger and shushed him. All of it was over now. The time had come to focus on finding Susan's doppelganger.

Dylan opened the door of his study and flicked on the light switch. Everything appeared normal, just as it had before the shadows invaded their lives. Dylan plopped onto his plush leather office-chair and fired up his desktop. He sat wondering why the rest of the team had experienced dire warnings regarding Susan and he had not. Had the shadows been more concerned with his lost memory and his predicament of missing time? Was his future just as ominous as Susan's?

The myriad icons on Dylan's desktop blinked as his computer awakened into full and thriving electronic life. While waiting, he became distracted by the EVP monitor next to the computer. He used the EVP device when he and the team explored the abandoned cemetery two nights ago. He'd set it down on his computer desk once he finally arrived home. There it remained for the past two days.

He stared at the handheld contraption, the latest in ghost-hunting technology. The EVP monitor and recorder was designed to detect, amplify, and record anomalous sounds. Walking through the Garden of the Weeping Angels with its thick, unkempt grass, Dylan had hoped to record any ghostly sounds unheard to the human ear. Sidney had listened with his clairaudient ear and heard the sounds of war in a distant past. Dylan wondered if any of those sounds were picked up by the EVP recorder.

He and the team had never found out. There hadn't been time to play back the EVP recording. They'd gone back to Brett's farmhouse afterward. Then, they'd learned the tragic news about Dean's daughter, Lydia. That's when things began to spiral out of their control. The next forty-eight hours happened so fast, the EVP device sat on his desk forgotten and ignored.

Tonight, Dylan had planned to continue writing the manuscript he was putting together about the Eagle Rock experience. He thought better of it as he stared at the EVP monitor. For all he knew, it contained an array of ghostly sounds unheard even by Sidney. Sitting in his plush swivel chair, he pushed himself away from the computer and over toward the device. After a quick inspection, he pressed the playback button and listened closely.

4

IN THE GLOW OF THE TORCH LIGHTS

THE VISION THE SHADOWS HAD SHOWN BRETT continued to haunt him. Through the wolf's crimson tainted view, a yellow streak had shimmered across a vast lawn. The wolf growled, bearing its fangs at the invisible entity. The vision depicted not only the well-groomed grass, but the copper-toned brick house situated upon it. It was Susan's house. Brett saw it clearly. Then the vision had ended.

Brett had spent his life overwhelmed by the skinwalker curse, but he was not a psychic. He was not prone to visions like Leah, or other-worldly sounds like Sidney. The shadows had planted a vision of the future in his mind, just as they had the rest of the team. Every member of the team had experienced replays of the past, and then revelations of the future. The futuristic visions depicted dark omens for both Susan and Dylan.

Tonight, Dylan had been the last to leave the farmhouse. Now, Brett and Tahoe remained sitting on the spacious back porch, reflecting, and basking in the glow of the patio torches Brett set up earlier. The night's events had worn Brett out, and because of his exhaustion, he couldn't help but notice the strange burst of energy that had taken hold of Tahoe. After his entanglement with the shadows, the old man seemed rejuvenated, energized, as if some unseen force had strengthened his soul. Brett said nothing. Maybe the evening's excitement left the old man wound up into what might become a sleepless night. Brett suspected that at Tahoe's age, living alone in the desert probably brought little excitement to his otherwise uneventful existence.

But now, dire warnings of the future took precedence over such trivialities.

"I think the strange moving entity I saw was Susan's doppelganger," Brett said. "I'm convinced I saw Susan's double in her ghostly form, gliding, or streaking across the lawn."

"If this is true," Tahoe said, "then there is a possible explanation. The doppelganger may seek to invade Susan's home. It would explain the face to face encounter I have foreseen."

Brett stirred in his seat, feeling the sunken weight of worry in his chest.

"I don't like these warnings about Susan. I think someone should stay with her."

Tahoe laughed. "I doubt your determined leader would allow it. I believe she somewhat welcomes a face to face confrontation with her mysterious double. Yet, you may be right. I believe Susan has been driven to desperation. She is now determined to destroy this doppelganger with her bare hands, a dangerous feat that may be easier said than done."

"Something else has me worried," Brett said. "You're aware of everything that happened after Uncle Jack died. Things are different now. In our therapy sessions, Susan has helped me contain my shifting to this property. It's part of being in control. Why would the wolf be at Susan's house? Why would I undergo the change somewhere else, unless I lacked control? I'm starting believe the vision could have also been a warning about me."

"An interesting theory, my friend." Tahoe's tone made him sound receptive, yet firm. "But there could be any reason the shifting would occur at Susan's house. Perhaps you are the one who ends up staying with her?" Brett hadn't even considered the possibility. Tahoe continued. "Never forget that while you are in control, my friend, absolute control is not possible. Your need to shift could still occur at any time and any place, just as it did the other night. You were here on your own property, but when you shifted into the form of the wolf, it did not stop the wolf from encountering the shadows. Remaining here at the farmhouse when the change occurs has provided you with a free pass, but what happens when the scenery changes? Surely, you cannot remain locked up here every night for the rest of your life, my friend."

Brett remained aware of this fact, but his adeptness at controlling his ability, or curse, however one looked at it, had allowed him to comfortably forget. Had the wolf been protecting Susan in the vision? It was possible. But until the moment occurred, all Brett and the rest of the team had were snippets and glimpses of ominous possibilities. The future is fleeting, until it becomes the present. And then the present is often too late, Brett thought.

Tahoe leaned forward. "I will describe for you exactly what I saw in my brief vision of Susan. But I warn you, there is not much to decipher."

———

EARLIER, TAHOE NOTICED THE TROUBLED LOOK ON Susan's face. He'd sat watching her, feeling the fear she emitted freely, a fear that remained with her even though the team's successes had been hard fought and won. Susan revealed that she could feel her doppelganger's presence out there somewhere. She needed to find her before it was too late.

Then, a flickering image wavered in and out of Tahoe's mind, a psychic itch that taunted him to scratch. Tahoe had closed his eyes and caught the image with his third eye. Two Susans stood staring at each other, yet only one of them was Susan Logan; the other was a fraud, a copy, a doppelganger. In the quick vision, Tahoe had been unable to tell them apart. Both Susans wore the same clothing. Tahoe was unable to see the background in the vision; it remained draped in a dim, shadowy fog. The two Susans had stood silently studying each other's faces.

"You will find her," Tahoe opened his eyes when the vision quickly faded. *"Soon."*

"So, that's what you saw tonight," Brett said.

"Susan knew that I was seeing something," Tahoe said. "I had to warn her, yet I didn't want to startle her. She and her dubious counterfeiter will meet face to face. That I have foreseen. What I cannot see is the end result. This has awakened a newfound fear inside me, one that has convinced me to extend my stay."

"We need you to stay, especially Susan," Brett reminded him. "That vision quest, or whatever you call it, we're hoping you and Leah will undergo it again, this time for Susan's sake." Tahoe understood this. He listened as Brett continued to revisit the night's events. "And you, you were unbelievable. It was as if some sort of spell came over you. It was everything, your vigor, the powerful stance you took against the shadows, even the booming thunder of your voice. It hadn't even sounded like you."

Brett was right in his estimation, and Tahoe knew why. Tonight, Sidney used the word "possessed," and used it precisely. Tonight, the spirit of Tahoe's great-grandfather, the warrior-chief, took possession of not only his body, but his soul. Tahoe remembered the chief's repeated admonition, spoken to him through dreams and visions.

"When the time comes, I will be there—inside you."

And that's exactly what the great chief had meant. Tahoe had felt it, a surge of electricity coursing through his body, as if he'd been struck by lightning. He'd risen up from the makeshift casket with an unfamiliar vigor, a much younger energy that was not his own. The world around him appeared clearer, more precise. Sharper, more vibrant hues burst with color before his eyes, yet the eyes were not his. The eyes were younger, fresher, and glimpsing the world without the dusty filter of age. Ancient words spouted from his lips, words Tahoe did not understand. Spells not of his own volition were cast and shouted with a commanding timbre.

Now, Tahoe couldn't help but ogle the burdensome puzzle box from the corner of his eye. It remained atop the picnic table in front of them. The team had unanimously decided that it was to be secretly buried in the woods adjacent to the farmhouse, where no one would ever find it. Brett noticed Tahoe eyeing the box. He reached his arm across the table and clamped his hand down upon it.

"I'm going to lock this in Uncle Jack's tool shed overnight. Tomorrow, I'll bury it in a spot only I will know about. Then, we'll be done with it forever. It's all right now, Tahoe. You'll never have to worry about the shadows again."

Tahoe looked at Brett, knowing this was true but silently pondering the change he felt taking place in his body. Since the incident earlier, his eyesight grew slowly sharper, more precise. He felt a younger spirit thriving within him. Even the arthritic pains in his muscles and joints seemed distant. A warm sensation of heat coursed through his veins. All of it probably amounted to nothing, possibly just an aftereffect of the spiritual invasion he'd experienced. The old chief's spirit had possessed of his body and left behind a lasting imprint like a supernatural resin. Tahoe would wake tomorrow as the achy old man he'd been for quite some years now.

"It's all yours," Tahoe said. He watched as Brett took the box and walked through the vast yard and up a small hill to the tool shed. He returned in minutes, having stored the box safely away. Brett yawned and decided to call it a night, but Tahoe had other plans. "Sleep soundly, my friend. I plan on sitting up for a while, if that's okay?"

"Fine by me," Brett said. "I'm not so sure any of us will be able to sleep tonight."

Tahoe laughed, suspecting Brett was right. They bid each other goodnight, and Tahoe sat alone, basking in the orange glow of the torch lights. A thousand crickets screeched around him, a collective cacophony reminding him of something, something he kept hearing over the past few days. Dusk had long since ushered in the chorus of crickets, but earlier, another sound preceded the repetitive screeching. Another school of insect sang their song from early in the afternoon until the crickets took the stage, a song slightly different than what he heard now. Tahoe heard them earlier, a sudden swarm whose sound came closer and closer. He heard them when they'd all traveled to the abandoned cemetery. The sound had been sudden, overwhelming, and as close to him as any of the shadows that watched in silent anonymity.

Cicadas. Tahoe could never remember the name for them, yet he did now, quickly like a young quiz master. The song of the cicadas always gave way to the chorus of crickets. That's the way it was here in the Pennsylvania countryside. But recently, Tahoe heard the cicadas like a thundering concerto all around him. At the time, he noticed, but remained quiet. Perhaps it had been the work of the shadows, but now Tahoe thought otherwise.

He heard something about cicadas long ago. They represented something not only in folklore and legend, but in literature as well. Tahoe never knew the whole story. Now, curiosity enveloped him.

He extinguished the torch lights and entered the house from the kitchen door, locking it behind him. Brett had gone to his room upstairs, leaving silence to permeate through the house. The dim blue glow emanating from the living room told Tahoe that as always, Brett's desktop computer remained on all night. Tahoe grimaced, thinking of the wasted electricity, but tonight such a flaw came in handy.

Tahoe was only moderately familiar with computers, yet he knew enough to search the internet. He often shunned internet research. Tahoe felt that none of it compared to a vast, physical library like he had in his Arizona home. Here in Pennsylvania, he was without his myriad volumes of legend, folklore, and history, his personal library where he spent hour after hour reading. But right now, Tahoe needed to search for only one word—cicadas.

He sat on the plush office chair of Brett's computer station and began typing into the search engine.

Cicadas, folklore and legend.

The results struck Tahoe. Long ago, he heard something similar to what the words on the bright white page boasted. He swallowed nervously as he read the results.

"In folklore and legends, cicadas are reported to represent rejuvenation, rebirth, and immortality."

Tahoe's eyes remained fixed on the words "rejuvenation" and "rebirth." He stared at the third word. Silent shock rippled through him. *Immortality.* His heart pounded vibrantly in his chest. Immortality. Tahoe laughed and thought better of it.

5

FRIDAY

She watched the sun rise, anxiously awaiting Susan's departure. Singular rays of sunshine sliced through the windows, and for a single instant, she became visible within the light. To the onlooker, she would have appeared as a ghost. She glided away from the light, mindful to avoid the windows in the daytime. Throughout the night, she'd lingered in her ghostly form, exploring the spacious house and even silently watching her host as she slept snuggly in her bed. Once Susan left in the morning, she would be free to thrive in her human form for at least eight hours. But today, the real Susan spoiled her plans.

She felt an indescribable reluctance, a sensation that didn't belong to her. Instinctively, she knew that Susan would stay home. Unseen, she moved away from the hallway window and watched as Susan descended the stairs. Susan wore a gray sweatshirt and sweatpants, most definitely not her hospital attire. Swiftly, she glided in her ghostly form and followed Susan into the kitchen. There, Susan prepared herself a steaming cup of black coffee and walked back down the hallway to her home office. Susan turned on her computer and sat in the plush chair behind her long mahogany desk. The doppelganger followed and sat in the chair opposite Susan's desk, continuing to silently watch her.

Susan picked up her desk phone and dialed a number. After a few seconds, she spoke to someone about her day's plans.

"That's right, Ashlee." She spoke into the receiver. "I've cleared my schedule for today. I had only one patient, and she was willing to reschedule. This past week has been somewhat trying, so I'm taking the day off. Should any emergencies arise, call me. I'll be here, at home."

Susan hung up the phone. Her silent double studied her every move: how she positioned her head while staring at the computer screen, how quickly she moved her hands while jostling items around on her desk and relocating them, and even how she pushed her glasses back up over the bridge of her nose with her finger. Her mind recorded Susan's actions like a video camera.

Another day of lingering in her ghostly form, another day of hiding within the shadowy dimness that lay just underneath the thriving pulse of the human world. Yet perhaps today would not be a total loss. Examining and studying her host, face to face, was exactly the type of research she needed to perfect her identity as Susan Logan. She looked upon her day's assignment as that of an understudy, learning from the original actor who would one day vacate the role. But Susan vacating her role was not an option. If Susan died, so did she, and replacing her would be a plan requiring years of work, thought, and time.

But she had all the time in the world. Susan was healthy, that she knew. How long would her initial plan to live as Susan in the daytime prevail? That remained to be seen. She hadn't even begun to experiment yet. Perhaps today, while Susan tapped away on her keyboard, she would materialize in another room—maybe the basement. She could penetrate the door leading down to the basement, glide freely down the stairs, and dwell in her human semblance while Susan remained upstairs.

After an hour of watching her host, she rose from the chair and moved swiftly past Susan's desk and through the open doorway of the small office. She glided through the hallway, making her way to the basement door.

———

SUSAN FELT A DRAFT BREEZE BY HER YET AGAIN. THIS time it couldn't have been a wayward gust that spiraled down the hearth. She looked around her. The peal of her desk phone made her stir in her seat. The loud bleating reminded her to lower the ring volume. She snatched up the receiver without glancing at the Caller ID and answered in her usual way. The voice on the other end provoked a nervous frenzy inside her.

"Susan, this is Tom Goddard."

She sat silently. A flutter of uneasiness swept her.

Tom Goddard, her detective friend, knew her and the team all too well. His suspicion had been immediately aroused after the Pittsburgh Police spotted her, Leah, and Sidney on Lydia's home video surveillance shortly before her death. Then, the Pittsburgh Police and a suspicious Tom badgered her about the visit to Lydia. Tom once helped the team into Cedar Manor for an investigation some years ago. He knew all too well how the real story of what happened in Cedar Manor was covered up; he was part of it. Now, Susan wondered if what had once been a beneficial connection was now boomeranging into a regrettable burden. What could he possibly want now?

"How may I help you, Tom?" Her tone was direct and straight to the point, unlike the bright, friendly tone she often used with him. He sighed before he spoke.

"I just wanted to let you know that Lydia Collier Valentine's body has been released to the funeral director." Susan stopped and stared blindly ahead, listening intently. "According to the autopsy results, there's no indication of foul play. All evidence points to an unfortunate accident."

Susan closed her eyes, knowing that Lydia's death was so much more than an accident. The shadows had caused Lydia's death. Dreadful words Susan could never tell Tom.

"So, I assume I'm off the hook?"

Goddard sighed. "No one was accusing you, Susan. They just wanted to know what happened while you visited only hours before."

"Still, I didn't like what's his face's tone." Susan referred to one of the Pittsburgh Police detectives who had come close to accusing her of wrongdoing.

"Look, I'm just glad that whatever you three were doing there had nothing to do with that young woman's death. And you know, if you need me for anything, that's why I'm here."

Silently, Susan scoffed. Someone like Goddard never could, nor would, believe all that she and the team had endured and encountered. Susan remained convinced that keeping him any closer as a confidant would shatter the team's wall of privacy and quickly dispel the difference between rumors and facts.

"Thank you, Tom, but I assure you all is well. I was simply researching a book and wanted more information about Dean Collier." Goddard remained silent. "I pray that Lydia rests in peace. I also pray for that family. They suffered Dean's suicide, and now this."

"I hear the viewing is on Sunday. I thought you might want to know."After Susan thanked him, he continued. "Oh, and another thing, there's something I forgot to mention. Let's just say this is off-the-record. When Forensics entered Lydia Valentine's bedroom, they noticed all the windows on that floor were shattered. No signs of a break-in or robbery. No cuts on Lydia's hands. It's as if the windows just shattered for no apparent reason. Interesting, isn't it?"

Susan sat silently, careful not to express herself in any way that would rouse his suspicion. She thought of the shadows and how they'd made physical contact in so many ways. Surely the shattered windows had been their work, efforts to frighten Lydia. The shadows had been masters of fear, terrifying with tactics she and the team had been made well familiar.

Susan reassured him that no potentially brewing storm existed. Soon, she replaced the receiver, forgetting all about the sudden draft that had swept by her. Turning her attention back toward the computer screen, she felt the distinct sensation of being watched.

Susan glanced around the room. Silly, she thought. She was alone in her own home. But after experiencing the terror of the shadows, instinctively, Susan rose from her chair, popped her head out the doorway, and peeked down the hall. Retreating back into the room, she leaned against the wall, wondering if she wasn't allowing fear to get the best of her. That was a possibility, but the feeling of being watched by invisible eyes remained.

————

THE SPIRIT AWOKE, LOST IN ITS CONFUSION. NOT MUCH time had passed. Now, it watched Susan as she sat behind her desk, talking into the phone. Her words caught its attention.

"I pray that Lydia rests in peace. I also pray for that family. They suffered Dean's suicide, and now this."

Dean's suicide. Susan's words brought back the small explosion, the sulfuric taste, and the vision of seeping blood.

Susan hung up the phone, stopped, and then glanced around the room. That's when the spirit neared her as closely as possible, close enough to feel the heat that radiated from her. That low-grade heat exuded from all living humans, but the last time the spirit watched Susan, it felt only coldness coming from her. Now, it seemed as if the hard shell had vanished.

The spirit lingered close enough to touch her shoulder. It reached out to touch her, to test how well it might slip into her body, how easily it might possess her. The low-grade heat, like a fever, climbed the closer the spirit got. The spirit's presence swept the softness of her skin. Then, Susan rose from the chair and walked over to the doorway. She gazed out into the hallway and turned back into the room, her mind pondering something the spirit couldn't read. The spirit could sense her vulnerability, her weakness. Now was not the time, but when the time came, it would exploit her weaknesses and invade her like a thief.

It would make its presence known. Then, it would consume her.

A sudden, inexplicable knowledge overwhelmed the spirit. Lydia. Susan had spoken her name. Emotions abounded: love, loss, grief, and pain. Lydia would be laid to rest—soon. Its rage, its revenge would have to wait. It would grieve its last physical connection to this world. Lydia's soul did not linger. She was not confined to this Earth. Her soul remained at rest. Yet the spirit would grieve. It would allow the abundance of raw emotions to fester. Then, it would be back for Susan. It would unleash its wrath upon her. But now, the spirit had somewhere to be.

6
———

A SATURDAY GATHERING

YESTERDAY, BRETT WOKE SHORTLY AFTER SUNRISE. Although he remained a night owl, Brett was no stranger to the sight of the morning sun as it rose up over the rural hills. He'd seen the magnificent spectacle many times. The early morning light was always best to see by, and he'd needed it for the task he performed soon after.

The shovels in Uncle Jack's tool shed leaned against the walls. He grabbed one of them, the biggest and heaviest shovel in the shed. A flurry of memories struck him as he gripped the handle, a fast moving flashback of a few years ago. This was the shovel he'd used to bury—he didn't want to think about that now. He set the shovel back against the wall and grabbed a lighter one. It would serve perfectly to bury the puzzle box. After all, he wasn't burying a body.

He plodded across the lawn, clenching the puzzle box in his left hand and toting the shovel with his right. He walked into the woods, the overhanging treetops instantly shading the world around him. Coolness swept him here in the thick greenery away from the sun. After a five minute walk through the woods, he arrived at a certain spot. It was a burial spot. Green had finally sprouted back over its baldness. He stopped for a moment and stared at it. Then, he shifted his eyes away and kept moving.

Approximately three hundred yards away, he stopped. He set the box down on the ground and plunged the shovel's spaded head into the earthen floor. Digging a hole three feet deep, he deemed it sufficient, and then wiped the sweat from his forehead. He placed the box inside the hole and buried it with the pile of dirt he'd excavated.

Finally, he packed the dirt with the back of the shovel and stood silently over the hole. The shadows were gone, along with the puzzle box. Only he knew the exact spot where the box was buried. The team had unanimously decided it was safer this way. Another chapter would remain buried here forever.

That was a little over twenty-four hours ago. He'd taken the time to tidy up the back patio. So much had gone on the last few days. Now, it appeared as it always did, without tables, chairs, and benches placed together for vision quests and phony wakes. Tahoe joined him on the back patio as the sun shined brightly through the countryside. The fresh flowery scent of late spring bloomed around them. The cicadas sang somewhat louder today.

Soon, Brett walked around to the front of the house and watched as Sidney's van pulled into the driveway. Sidney and Susan emerged from the van's front doors; Dylan and Leah exited from the back. Another Saturday gathering with the team, Brett thought. Imagining the worst was buried behind him, Brett wondered what today would bring.

———

TAHOE AWOKE AN HOUR EARLIER TODAY. ABSENT WAS the slight grogginess he routinely felt upon waking. He rose from the bed and planted his feet on the floor. It took him a few moments to realize that he'd done this without the dull ache in his lower back or the sore arthritic pains in his legs. His body was up and moving before any of it registered in his mind. Tahoe knew what he felt like. He hadn't experienced his current physical prowess in over twenty-five years. He continued to ignore it as he showered, dressed, and traipsed downstairs to the kitchen.

Perhaps it was the fresh country air, the invigorating breeze that swept the countryside. Living in the desert, he hadn't been used to this weather with its pleasantly warm days and cool windswept nights. Perhaps the desert heat had finally taken its toll upon his aging body, which was now responding differently to the climate change. Either way, it was unimportant now. The team would be here soon.

In the kitchen, Tahoe and Brett scarfed down a quick breakfast of eggs, toast, and coffee. Moments later, Brett stepped out onto the patio. Soon, Tahoe joined him.

The spring sunshine bathed the world around him in a magnificent orange glow. It beamed brightly, kissing the green grass, the house's red siding, and the overlapping hills in the distance. The scent of blooming flora thrived. The sky appeared as a baby blue sea, and fluffy white clouds swam slowly across it.

Beholding the optical splendor, Tahoe heard a sound coming closer. Not quite the same as the nighttime screeching, but a repetitive, up and down clamor, one that grew louder and surrounded him out here on the patio.

The cicadas were singing to him. He kept quiet and slowly followed Brett around the side of the house and to the driveway. The team had arrived in Sidney's van. He would maintain his focus and forget about the thundering cicadas.

———

DYLAN WALKED WITH THE REST OF THE TEAM THROUGH Brett's driveway and around to the back patio, carrying the EVP monitor with him. As chief-investigator, he planned to begin today's meeting. The evidence he brought would need to be heard first and foremost. Once they were all seated on the patio, he turned to Susan.

"Susan, I'd like to begin the meeting, if I may. What I have to say is urgent." Susan agreed. Dylan stood at the end of the long picnic table, and then set the EVP device down in front of him. Then, he began. "As you all remember, I brought this EVP recorder with us to the Garden of the Weeping Angels. I heard something on the playback, something that's going to shock everyone here." Dylan paused, and then turned to Susan. "Especially you."

He noticed them ogling the handheld device that resembled a transistor radio. Sidney rose from his seat and leaned over the device.

"You picked up EVP's that day?"

"More than a few," Dylan replied. "I need you to listen closely to this playback, Sid. You were 'listening' that day. Maybe you can identify the sounds that were recorded."

Sidney sat back down and scooted his seat in closer toward the device.

"No doubt," he said. "I won't forget those sounds anytime soon."

"I'm going to play this back at the highest possible volume without encountering distortion." Dylan continued. "Still, I need all of you to listen very closely."

Dylan pressed a button on the side of the device. Static crashed and died away in the briefness of seconds. The echoing sound of an active recording captivated their attentions. Cicadas sang in the captured background. And then came the soft thrashing of light footsteps trudging through the grass.

"That sound is me walking through the cemetery," Dylan pointed out. "As expected, our own sounds were picked up in the background. This is why we need to listen closely."

A repetitive clicking roused curiosities.

"What's that sound?" Leah asked.

"That's Susan taking pictures with my camera," Brett said.

Dylan confirmed this. Then, Leah's voice was heard faintly in the background.

"Walk with me, Sidney, like we always do. I see. You listen."

"That was just before we walked together through the cemetery," Sidney said.

Leah nodded.

"Get ready," Dylan warned.

Suddenly, the sound of an explosion obliterated the mundane whisperings of their outing.

"*KAPOW!*"

Startled in their seats, they exchanged glances.

"That's the explosion I heard," Sidney said.

The explosive clamor reverberated, causing a slight strain of static that quickly faded. Brief silence ensued, except for the sound of cicadas in the background. But the quiet was again interrupted. The rapid exchange of gunfire became hauntingly clear. Then, ghostly shouting mingled amid the clamor. Much of it remained indiscernible, but not all of it. One word escaped the cloudy depths of Elysium. It was shouted with a ghostly roar.

"*FIRE!*"

Again, eruptions of gunfire boomed from the small device. Some of them boasted bigger and louder than others, but clearly gunfire, clearly the sounds of war.

"Those were the sounds I heard," Sidney said. He closed his eyes, remembering. "Yet I heard them much more distinctly."

The captured sounds were brief, rapid interruptions of the living realm and ceased just as quickly as they'd been heard. Now the sounds faded back into Elysium, eternally sentenced to recur over and over again. Once again, the team heard the soft thrashing of Dylan's footsteps, the low intermingling of voices, and the light breeze that whistled in the recording. The camera's clicking resumed in the background.

"Focus your attentions on the clicking of the camera," Dylan advised. "Wait for the sound that overlaps it. It sounds as if it's drawn to the clicking."

Dylan didn't want to say more. He didn't want to influence or manipulate what they heard. When the upcoming sound occurred, it would be abundantly clear if they all heard the same thing. He would wait for the sound and watch their reactions, especially Susan's. The camera continued clicking.

CLICK-CLACK, CLICK-CLACK, CLICK-CLACK.

Then, a low guttural moan erupted, overwhelming the clicking in the background. A ghostly voice made its presence known.

"SU-SAN..."

Gasps erupted around the table. Dylan watched as the color drained from Susan's face. Planting her hands firmly on the table, Susan rose into a standing position and trembled.

A GHOSTLY VOICE CALLED OUT HER NAME. SHE WAS sure of it. Susan heard her name clearly spoken on the EVP recording. The gasps of shock around her confirmed it. She felt her body turn cold, the chills rippling up her spine. Her legs felt numb, restless. She had to stand, anything to escape the gripping shock. Rising from her seat, she shook, as if an unseen hand reached out from the grave and touched her. Susan looked to Dylan, her heart pounding.

"Who, or what, was that?"

"I know you all heard what I heard," Dylan said. "Susan, someone or something called out your name. Obviously, it was none of us. Did everyone else hear the same thing?"

Heads nodded. Susan took a deep breath and sat back down.

"Dylan, play that back again," she said.

Dylan pressed another button on the device, eliciting a zipping, twisting sound as the recording rewound. Again, he pressed playback.

Once again, the rapid clicking resumed. For a second time, Susan heard the ghostly call of her name, but this time she listened to the sound of the voice. The voice sounded warbled, warped, dragging out the two syllables of her name.

"SU-SAN..."

The voice she could not identify, yet the sound of it touched her deeply inside, somehow leaving its mark on her soul.

"That voice," Susan began. "I can't—" She gasped, at a loss of words. Her mind drew a blank, leaving her unable to finish her thought.

"Do you recognize the voice?" Leah asked.

"No, it's impossible." Susan thought for a moment. "Sidney, you heard the shadows speak. Is this voice the same as what you heard?" She pointed to the EVP device. "Is this the voice of one of the shadows?"

"The voice I recall was soft, yet raspy." Sidney shrugged. His eyes twitched in skepticism. "This voice is not quite the same as what I heard when the shadows spoke to me."

"Could it possibly be her, my doppelganger?"

"I doubt that," Brett answered. "If she were watching, lingering around at the cemetery in her ghostly form, then why would she not reveal herself?"

"That would defeat her purpose of remaining hidden," Tahoe said.

"So then why call out Susan's name at all?" Sidney wasn't convinced either.

"I agree," Dylan said. "I think this is something else." He glanced at Susan. "Would you like to hear it again?"

"No, that's quite enough," she said. Susan turned to Tahoe and Leah. "This thing that called out to me, whatever it is, is it still around me? Do either of you see anything?"

Tahoe closed his eyes as he spoke. "That day in the cemetery, I remember focusing with my third eye. Like Leah, I saw the scenes of war, but not much else." He opened his eyes. "I see nothing attached to you now."

"Same here," Leah said. "Tahoe and I will embark upon another vision quest. We're going to try and flesh the doppelganger out, so to speak."

"And if that doesn't work?" Susan asked.

"Then we wait for her to appear," Brett said.

Susan lowered her head and sighed. Secretly, she felt the past year taking its toll, but she was their leader. Crumbling under the enormity of such an invisible weight was not an option. She changed the subject, anything to forget the ongoing tension she felt.

"I heard from Goddard yesterday," she said. "The police have released Lydia's body. Her viewing is tomorrow. I'm not so sure it's a good idea to attend."

"Why not?" Sidney demanded. "It's imperative that either you, or all three of us, attend in order to show our innocence, even if we are somewhat guilty."

"Sid's right in his offhand way," Leah said. "If we stay behind, we confirm any suspicions surrounding us. Lydia's husband, Parker, already knows we were there. It becomes even more suspicious if we don't extend our condolences."

Suddenly, Susan didn't feel much like their leader anymore. Leah and Sidney were making more sense than her. Of course she had to attend Lydia's viewing, but the guilt she felt was crippling. The three of them would go tomorrow and display their sorrows. It was the least they could do. Susan remembered the rest of the conversation she had with Goddard.

"There's more," she said. "Goddard revealed something to me yesterday, off-the-record. All the windows on Lydia's second floor were shattered. The police cannot explain why."

Glances exchanged. Eyes met, conveying the same expressions of unspoken agreement.

"Interesting," Dylan said. "Undoubtedly the work of the shadows."

Susan noticed that Tahoe had closed his eyes for a brief second, and then opened them again. She saw the look of confusion on his face. His eyes narrowed in speculation.

"Perhaps," he said. "What I see is unclear."

"During the last vision quest, we saw what happened to Lydia," Leah said. "We saw no windows breaking."

"Not that it matters, now." Sidney's tone was bitter. He turned to Susan. "So, we will attend Lydia's viewing tomorrow, right?" Sidney made it sound more like an order than a question. Susan agreed.

Then, Tahoe lifted his head slightly upward, listening to the singing cicadas.

"Shh," he said. "Do you hear that?"

Susan and the others glanced at each other.

"The cicadas?" Susan asked. "What about them?"

Tahoe slowly turned his gaze outward, listening but saying nothing. Susan noticed the awestruck look on his face. She wondered not only what he was hearing, but what visions passed through the great seer's mind in this moment.

"I'm not hearing anything," Sidney said, "other than cicadas."

Tahoe turned his head quickly back and forth again, shaking the puzzled expression from his face and sighing. He turned to Leah and took her hand.

"I think it is time to attempt our journey," he said. He gazed out upon the vast rural countryside, his eyes squinted. "The images are there. They are trying to show themselves, but we must look for them." He turned back to Leah, squeezing her hand. "Are you ready, Little One?"

She nodded. "I'm ready."

7

VISION SEEKERS

THE CICADAS' SONG ASCENDED TO A THUNDERING chorus, yet only Tahoe could hear the heightening crescendo. He gripped Leah's left hand firmly. She equally clasped his right. Having set up two chairs once again on the northern side of the patio, they faced each other as they had only days ago. Only now they weren't seeking the origin of the shadows through random visions of history. Now, they sought to envision any glimpse or sign of a woman who lived as the exact copy of Susan, who sat only inches away, watching them.

Tahoe and Leah closed their eyes, their hands clasped firmly together. They focused on their third eyes, the areas directly in the middle of their foreheads. They gazed into the vision world as they would normally do on their own, individually. But this time, as last time, they merged their third eyes together as one. The objective was not a trick, but a strange glitch they would both try and catch, like both of them jumping onto a runaway train at the same time. They fell into a trance, their arms locked together at the hands.

Suddenly Leah saw Tahoe standing before her, but not in this world, in the visionary realm she and Tahoe had just entered. This time, there was no beautiful, bountiful desert set against a multi-colored horizon. She and Tahoe stood surrounded by the mist that had enveloped them throughout the course of their last journey. Leah looked around her.

"It seems different this time," she said.

"And it should be, Little One. We seek answers at a different time, for a different reason."

Leah referred to the absence of the desert, and the vivid past and present scenes that had once set a stage for them. But just as she spoke, the mist began to evaporate in swirls around them. Instantly, the vision world displayed a background, one that resembled the rural setting they sat transfixed in. Tahoe still stood in front of her, but behind him, rolling hills abounded and overlapped each other. Spring buds bloomed to life in vibrant yellows, whites, reds, and pinks. Leah heard a soft, pleasant fluttering that increased in volume. Then she saw them, cicadas, by the thousands.

They surrounded Tahoe in the vision world. They swarmed the hills in multitudes, leaving no bare spot uncovered. She saw them everywhere, seeming to pay homage to Tahoe as if he represented them.

"I've never seen so many cicadas," Leah said. *"It's as if they're drawn to you."*

Tahoe looked at her with a blank expression. He seemed to somehow understand but not completely. Then, Leah his saw his face change. In the flash of a second, she saw the great chief, Tahoe's great-grandfather. The chief's face formed over Tahoe's. She watched Tahoe's lines and wrinkles melt away and morph into the younger chief's face, and then back again. It was a hint, a sign.

"Tahoe, your face—"

"There's no time, Little One." He interrupted her, pointing his finger in the opposite direction. *"The scene is changing. Look!"*

———

STUNNED BY THE SIGHT OF THE SWARMING CICADAS

that surrounded him, Tahoe stayed silent as their volume climaxed into a thundering chorus. Leah saw the same thing. Their chakras merged, and now they stood in the vision world they had sought. The sudden vivacity he felt in this moment strengthened as the cicadas' song climbed in volume. Tahoe could feel the presence of the chief by the much youthful vigor that thrived within him. Then, Leah said something about his face. There was no time to explain to her what he had yet to understand. The scene in the vision world they inhabited began to change. An image was forming.

"Look!" Tahoe pointed behind her.

In a sweeping horizontal motion, a wall formed in front of them. For a moment the wall seemed solid, and then not solid. In the blink of an eye, the wall was visible in its wet cement form. Something moved within the wall. Tahoe and Leah watched as a shape seemingly swam in an almost slithering motion, parting atoms and molecules. A featureless face formed in the wall and then disappeared. Then, the wall became solid again.

"What is that?" Just as Leah spoke, the wall faded.

"Like most things we see here, Little One, it is a sign."

Tahoe's words reminded him of the cicadas, but this thought was interrupted by a wavering image. The image developed slowly, becoming clearer and clearer until it revealed two identical women, two Susans, staring directly at each other.

"There!" Leah reacted, pointing to what they saw.

"It is the same as what I saw in the vision, two of them, meeting face to face."

Suddenly, Leah gasped.

"I want to psychically latch on to one of them, but which one's which?"

"A good question, Little One."

The two Susan's remained identical. Unlike the moment when Leah first encountered Susan's doppelganger, this time, there appeared to be no difference. The women faced each other, dressed in exactly the same clothing.

"I think the one on the left is Susan's doppelganger," Leah said. *"I'm going to try and see further."*

Leah moved toward the vision. Tahoe called out behind her.

"Wait, Little One!"

Abruptly they awoke. Their arms collapsed in a swaying motion, their interlocking grip suddenly broken. Tahoe and Leah slumped backwards in their chairs. Tahoe let out a sigh. Then, he sat up and glanced at the others who sat watching.

"The bond was broken," he said.

"I apologize," Leah said, gripping the sides of the chair. "That was my fault."

"You were too anxious to see. But not to worry, we did see *something.*"

"Only three minutes this time." Brett recorded this second vision quest. "So, what exactly did you both see?"

Tahoe told them about the wall, and how something or someone moved within it.

"Then, the wall vanished," Leah said. "It was replaced by the image of two identical Susans. I tried to focus on which one was the doppelganger. When I tried to get closer to the image, I broke the vision quest." Again, Leah apologized.

"The wall," Brett said. "These doppelgangers move through walls. That was how Angus Marlowe entered the Page residence six months ago."

"That's right," Dylan added. "We watched Taryn move through a wall."

"So, you think she's going to move through walls to get to me?" Susan asked.

"This is why I've been so adamant to see you safely inside the house." Sidney raised his voice slightly, his words bearing down on Susan. "We discussed this possibility earlier."

"You mean my house?" Susan sounded skeptical. "You all think she's going to move through the walls of my house to get to me?" She shook her head. "I've seen nothing unusual in the house since I witnessed the shadows."

"I still think someone should stay with you," Leah said. "You shouldn't be in that house alone."

"I'll be fine," Susan replied. "Besides, so far she's been running from us, hasn't she? It's *we* who are trying to find *her*. And remember, should anything happen to me, she would succumb also. As I've said before, I'm anxious to meet her face to face. I plan on ending this once and for all."

"That's what we're afraid of," Tahoe said.

———

LEAH KEPT THINKING ABOUT THE SWARM OF CICADAS that surrounded Tahoe in the vision quest. By Tahoe's own admission, everything seen in the vision world was a sign, a message. Leah never mentioned the cicadas, or the fact that afterward, Tahoe had remained silent about that part of their psychic journey. She saw no negative implications when she witnessed the swarm and their obvious attraction to Tahoe. The surrounding scene had thrived with beauty and life. Then, Tahoe's face changed into the chief's. What could it all have meant?

Now, as nightfall descended, she readied for bed, anxious to delve into a psychological thriller that recently caught her eye in the bookstore. Suddenly, a vision overcame her. She dropped the book on her bed and closed her eyes.

She saw Susan, or was it Susan's doppelganger? The same ghastly figure she'd envisioned a few nights ago stood before her, bearing Susan's face yet with a forlorn raggedness and a stark, menacing stare. Bloodshot eyes seeped red-tinged wetness. The figure walked toward her in the vision, but this time something was different. A grimy, yellowish-brown tint surrounded this being that bore Susan's semblance. Then the figure stopped, arms outstretched, and opened its mouth. Tilting its head backward, a raspy wheeze escaped the figure as it exhaled. From within, a mist of the same yellowish-brown color spewed outward like the angry breath of a volcano.

Possessed. Intuition inserted the word into Leah's mind automatically. Then, the vision was gone, replaced by the blackness of closed eye lids.

Leah opened her eyes and plopped down on the bed, troubled by what she'd just seen. She hadn't searched for this image; it found her, as if the images in the broken vision quest had somehow continued. Leah had seen something malevolent inhabiting the figure in the last vision. Possessed? Susan? By what or whom? In its own way the vision didn't make sense. Susan's doppelganger was not a demon; she was unable to possess Susan. What about the strange, yellowish-brown hue that tainted the vision?

She sat and tried to make sense where none could be found. She sighed in frustration, opting to mention it to Tahoe later. Leah slipped into bed, hoping to read, but her thoughts became hauntingly distracted.

———

TAHOE SAW A ROOM FULL OF PEOPLE.

The vision was sudden, overcoming him while he sat on the northern side of the back patio gazing up at the plethora of stars that filled the nighttime sky. So sudden that it seemed as if the broken vision quest had abruptly continued, interrupting the tranquility of this peaceful moment to finish telling a foreboding tale. He closed his eyes against the splendorous eruption of stars above and allowed the vision to play out.

A parlor of some kind. Casually dressed men and women stood idly chatting and congregating in this room filled with flowers and pictures. Blurriness hindered the view of the pictures that seemed somewhat far away. Tahoe's third eye moved through the crowd until it came to a casket. Inside, a young woman slept eternally. How beautiful she was. Long red hair framed her sweet heart-shaped face. Tahoe turned his sight away from the sleeping beauty and back toward the crowd.

He saw Susan shaking hands with a dark-haired woman. Leah and Sidney stood behind her. Something hung in the air above Susan and the dark-haired woman, a lingering mist. Yet something disturbed Tahoe about the mist. It was a sickly, yellowish-brown haze clinging thickly to the air itself. Tahoe saw it for what it was —a leftover spiritual resin. Words formed in Tahoe's mind: bad, unclean, and worst of all, unholy.

Susan and the dark-haired woman spoke casually, their expressions somber and heartbroken. Tahoe watched as the yellowish-brown haze engulfed the dark-haired woman. Suddenly, Tahoe saw blood streaking the dark-haired woman's face and hands. Then, the vision quickly changed.

Two Susans faced each other once again, yet Tahoe failed to see a background setting. The yellowish-brown mist surrounded Susan and her doppelganger, darkening in color until it consumed the both of them. Then, the vision ended. Tahoe saw nothing but blackness.

He opened his eyes. Brett, who had been focusing his telescope in the yard, now stood over him as he sat idly in his chair.

"Are you okay?"

"The vision quest Leah and I embarked upon earlier was not completed," Tahoe answered him. "So, the visions decided to find me. I suspect the same has happened to Leah."

Tahoe described the vision of the funeral parlor, the casket, and the young, redheaded female inside it.

"Lydia," Brett concluded.

"Such a beautiful young woman, but I'm afraid there was more to the vision." Tahoe told him about seeing Susan, as well as the dark-haired woman, and the dirty, yellowish-brown haze that hung in the air around them. The dark-haired woman, covered in blood. "This is most troubling. I'm unable to see what this mist or haze has to do with Susan's double."

"You said a yellowish-brown haze?" Brett stroked his chin. Tahoe nodded. "That reminds me of the vision the shadows planted in my mind, the wolf chasing the yellow streak through Susan's yard."

Tahoe glanced at him. Brett had made a connection. He knew it.

"The haze resembled an unclean spirit," Tahoe said. "Yet the visions remain confusing. I am certain that the unclean spirit was *not* that of the young woman in the casket. So, am I to assume that whatever this thing is, this tainted force, is an altogether different manifestation than Susan's doppelganger? Is the doppelganger responsible for this mysterious spiritual occurrence?" Tahoe sighed. "There is no way to be sure."

"Let's not drop this on Susan tonight," Brett suggested. "She has enough to worry about right now. I can see the fear on her face, though she hides it well."

"She needs to remain aware of her surroundings at the funeral parlor. She needs to stay vigilant and watchful, especially of this dark-haired woman. I'll call her in the morning."

Tahoe would also call Leah and ask her what she saw. They both had ventured into the vision world. They both provoked that which had yet to occur. The visions continued to play out to the both of them. Tahoe could feel it, that and something else.

After seeing the vision of the funeral parlor, Tahoe felt a sudden foreboding, a great darkness eclipsing inside of him, one that made him tremble inside. Tahoe suspected that the strange misty haze remained a separate entity that manifested of its own volition. The yellowish-brown color of the haze signified something bad and impure, something malevolent. But time would shed light in its direction.

8

THE FUNERAL PARLOR

Susan opened her eyes on Sunday morning, dreading the thought of meeting Lydia's family, not to mention seeing that innocent young woman dead in a casket. But Sidney and Leah were right; they had to make an appearance. She breakfasted and showered quickly, then chose the finest ensemble from her wardrobe.

She had a little extra time before Sidney and Leah picked her up in the van. The ride into Pittsburgh would take at least forty-five minutes. She slipped into her home office and sat behind her desk. Her hands searched beneath the top of the desk until locating a key taped underneath. The small silver key opened a bottom desk drawer she kept locked at all times. Susan turned the key inside the lock, eliciting a light metallic pop. She opened the drawer and retrieved a small, gray, metal box.

She never told anyone about this secret box she kept locked away. Regardless of her top-notch security system, she remained a single, older woman, alone in this big house. What if one day her top-notch security system failed? Thankfully, she'd never needed to use what was secretly stashed inside, but unknown to everyone who knew her; she *did* know how to use it.

Susan lifted the cover of the small metal box and examined its contents. The revolver's gunmetal gray glimmered in the gleam of her desk lamp. She'd learned how to use it at the shooting gallery just after acquiring her gun owner's permit. From then on, it remained here, locked away in the unlikely event of an emergency.

It wasn't so long ago that as a psychiatrist, she would have diagnosed any of her patients as overcompensating, luring themselves into a false sense of security, but after her confrontation with the Men in Black last year, she was taking no chances. After her experience in the blue realm, she longer believed in a false sense of security.

Tahoe and Leah thought her doppelganger might attempt to infiltrate her home. If that was true, then Susan would be ready for her. She told them she would end this once and for all, and that's exactly what she meant. Like the rest of the team, Susan remembered what happened to Angus Marlowe and Taryn Page. The same would happen with her doppelganger. She would fade away into her ghostly form without a trace. Susan would get away with such a murder, and the knowledge that she reveled in this fact slightly frightened her. Yet helplessness left her with no other choice.

Suddenly, her phone rang.

———

WHEN TAHOE DESCRIBED HIS LATE-NIGHT VISION, IT intensified the apprehension Leah already felt. He phoned her early this morning, asking if she experienced visions the night before. She'd described last night's vision to him, specifically the yellowish-brown haze that expelled from the seemingly possessed figure.

"It is even worse than I feared," Tahoe said.

The memory of this morning's conversation paused in Leah's mind as Sidney pulled into Susan's driveway. Once Susan got into the van, and they were en route to Pittsburgh, Leah would fill her in on the details of her vision. She and Sidney waited less than a minute. Finely clad in a silver pants-suit and matching jacket, Susan exited the house, descended the front stairs to the driveway, and climbed into the van.

"So, I need to remain watchful today, according to Tahoe." Susan spoke suddenly after sliding the van's door shut. "He phoned me just before you both arrived. Apparently, I may have something else to worry about other than *her*."

Leah related the details of her own vision. "I don't want you to be frightened. I saw the ghastly image of you again, arms outstretched, bloodshot eyes, same as the vision the shadows had shown me. But this time, I also saw the dirty, yellowish-brown haze that Tahoe mentioned. The figure exhaled this strange mist, as if it had been inhabited by it."

A silent pause ensued. Leah could feel the tension created by her words.

"You mean *possessed* by it," Susan concluded.

"The vision was difficult to interpret," Leah added. "I don't want to draw inaccurate conclusions, but Tahoe saw the haze or mist surrounding both you and your doppelganger. He sees it as some type of unseen force, something that clings to both of you."

"He believes that whatever this mist or haze represents is something separate from your doppelganger." Sidney stressed this point, but Susan had already been warned.

"I wonder if this *thing* has to do with the voice that called out my name on the EVP."

"That's entirely possible," Sidney said.

Susan laughed, nervously. "So, I'm about to be possessed by what, a ghost?"

"See, that's just it," Leah stressed. "None of it makes any sense at this point in time. Tahoe and I have glimpsed only bits and pieces, scattered fragments of a futuristic puzzle. The vision quest was broken, and that's my fault."

"None of this is your fault, Leah," Susan replied. "I'm ready to deal with *her*, one way or another. When she shows herself, she will cease to be a problem. Afterward, whatever comes this way," Susan paused. "Let it come."

Leah turned her head toward Sidney, fearing the worst.

———

THE ZACHARY HARMON FUNERAL PARLOR APPEARED exactly as Tahoe had described it to her, so much so that Susan felt the sudden sway of dizziness. A cornucopia of roses, carnations, violets, and lilies were just a few of the flowers amassed in arrangements, perfuming the air with an almost distracting aroma. The pictures Tahoe failed to clearly visualize were collages of images posted together on wide poster boards. Lydia's wedding. Lydia as a teenager. Lydia as a child. Lydia as a newborn. Pictures of Dean. A young Dean Collier held his infant daughter on his lap and stared back at Susan from the photograph.

A chill swept her spine. She turned away from the poster boards and clustered closely to Leah and Sidney who stood behind her.

"Come on," she said. "Let's do this as quickly as possible."

"Don't be nervous," Sidney advised. "It's starting to show."

Several mourners blocked Susan's view of the casket, as a line of people stood waiting to pay their final respects. Susan, Sidney, and Leah stood patiently together. The few quiet moments gave Susan a chance to collect herself. She hadn't expected to see Dean's piercing green eyes suddenly glimpse back at her from the picture, but they had. The moment haunted her, a sudden reminder that her worst failure would always be there, staring back at her.

Ahead of them, mourners prayed and passed to the right, where they greeted Lydia's family. As they did so, the inside of the casket came closer and closer into view. Soon, the three of them stood looking down at Lydia in the white casket with gold trim. The beautiful young woman she'd met only days ago lay in eternal slumber, forever clad in a white silk dress, her long red hair hanging in tresses down to her hands which clasped a crucifix.

Susan took a deep breath.

"I'm so sorry, Lydia," she whispered.

Sidney wrapped his arm around her shoulder and squeezed tightly, a silent warning that they were being observed. Susan glanced from the corner of her eye. Several of Lydia's family members stood watching them, even as they accepted condolences from passing guests. Susan didn't look directly at them, but she sensed their lingering stares, their ardent curiosity.

Susan nodded to Leah and Sidney, signaling that is was time to meet the grieving family, awkward or not. They stepped away from the casket and off to the right like the others before them. A tall, young man in his thirties, with blondish-brown hair and blue eyes, sporting a clean-cut yuppie look, simply stared at them as they approached. Susan could see the devastation on his face. As a psychiatrist, she recognized that faraway look of shock, one that revealed how the mind questioned whether or not the current reality was real. He was Lydia's husband.

"I'm Doctor Susan Logan," she said to him, extending her hand. She apologized for his loss. "I was a friend of Lydia's father."

Something stopped her from saying more. She watched his expression zero in on her as he shook her hand, as if the fog in his mind had suddenly lifted.

"Yes, you came to visit Lydia that day," he said. "I'm her husband, Parker." He drew a sharp intake of breath, having referred to his wife in the present tense.

Susan saw the woman with dark hair step forward and stare at her. She stood waiting for the woman to approach her. No doubt she was Lydia's mother, the infamous Lauren. Susan maintained her focus on Parker. There was something she needed to say.

"I can't begin to tell you how much I wish I'd stayed that day."

Parker thanked her. "I'm glad she got to talk about her Dad. She loved him so much."

Susan introduced Sidney and Leah, who extended their

condolences. Then, Susan turned to face the dark-haired woman. Susan could see that she had once been beautiful. Her shoulder-length dark hair remained thick and wavy and sported wisps of gray at her temples. Susan marveled at her exotic blue eyes, big rounded orbs which seemingly hypnotized.

Susan shook her hand, introduced herself, and once again extended her sorrow.

"You must be Lydia's mother," she said.

"Yes, I'm Lauren Kessler." She spoke with an even, flat tone. Between the sound of Lauren's voice and her undeterred staring, Susan sensed a level of curiosity coming from her that bordered on suspicion. "So, you were a friend of Dean's?"

Susan felt the same chill that gripped her only moments ago. Suddenly, she remembered Tahoe's vision. Distracted, Susan glanced up and around her. No strange haze or mist clung to the air. Still, this moment felt like déjà vu. Sidney and Leah cast stares at her, silent pleas that urged her to stay focused.

"Yes, many years ago," Susan answered. "It was an honor to finally meet your daughter. My heart goes out to you."

Lauren nodded. "Thank you." She spoke calmly, dragging the two words out, yet her tone sounding as if her curiosity had finally segued into suspicion.

Not wanting this conversation to go further, especially within earshot of strangers, Susan motioned to Leah and Sidney with her eyes. As Leah and Sidney approached Lauren to pay their respects, an older woman tapped Lauren on the shoulder from behind. Susan felt the hard weight of tension evaporate inside her as Lauren turned away and hugged the woman. The woman must have been a close family friend. She clutched Lauren tightly, sobbing loudly in disbelief.

Susan stepped toward Leah and Sidney. She grabbed Sidney's arm.

"Let's get lost for a few respectful moments, and then get out of here," she said.

"Sounds good," Sidney said in a lowered voice. "I gotta find the john anyway."

"Wonderful, Sidney, but please make it quick."

Sidney found the restroom after they stepped into a narrow hallway. Susan and Leah casually entered another room, a lounge, where several guests gathered for coffee, cookies, and conversation. Susan craned her neck, peering out into the room they'd just left, making certain that Lauren hadn't followed them. Susan had worried that Parker would have been the first to make some crazy accusation about their being the last to see Lydia alive, outside of Mrs. Morris, the maid. He hadn't, but Susan remained unconvinced that Lauren was capable of the same lack of suspicion or blame. The last thing Susan or the team needed was public attention.

Susan was relieved when Sidney appeared around the corner and entered the room. "Great," she whispered. "Now, let's casually walk toward the door."

Only a few steps away, they passed through a doorway leading out into the front hall. The doorman nodded to Susan as he opened the front door for the three of them. Gratefully, Susan, Leah, and Sidney stepped outside onto the funeral parlor's front terrace. They were about to descend the stairs to the parking lot when a voice called out from behind them.

"Excuse me, Doctor Logan?"

Susan's heart sunk. She turned and faced Lauren, who had followed them outside.

"Yes, Mrs. Kessler?"

"Please, call me, Lauren," she said. "I was wondering if I might have a word with the three of you before you leave."

Now, Susan heard no suspicion in Lauren's tone, only curiosity.

"Sure," Susan said. "Why don't we step over here?"

They moved away from the front door, out of the path of exiting guests, and then converged at the far end of the spacious terrace. Chairs and a couch were set up for guests, but Susan stood firmly, not anticipating a long discussion. Lauren shot a quick glance over her shoulder, obviously not wanting to be overheard.

"Please forgive me if I sound nosy or speak out of turn," Lauren began. "I just want to know. Is it true the three of you are paranormal investigators?"

Susan braced herself, but the fact that they were paranormal investigators was no longer a secret. Lydia had researched them on the internet after they left her home. The police discovered it when they searched the house, and Lydia's computer, after the incident. Somewhat relieved, Susan took a deep breath before she answered.

"Yes, we are in fact, paranormal investigators."

Lauren's eyebrows bridged together, an unconscious display of her heightening curiosity. Susan could see that something stirred in her mind.

"What I'd really like to know is—why did my daughter contact you?"

Susan explained that Lydia had not contacted them. *She* contacted Lydia. Lauren interrupted before Susan could elaborate.

"You said you were a friend of Dean's." Then, after a slight pause, she lowered her voice. "Did it have anything to do with the incident in Dean's childhood?"

Susan began answering Lauren's question before realizing she'd been taken by surprise.

"No, you see, I'm also a psychiatrist. Leah and Sidney, here, are my researchers. I wanted to speak to Lydia about Dean's condition."

"I see," Lauren replied. Susan noticed the puzzled look on her face, as if accidentally, Lauren *had* spoken out of turn. "So, Lydia *didn't* contact you about her father?"

Again, Susan affirmed that she hadn't. Now, the bridge of Lauren's eyebrows lowered in confusion. She stared off in wonder for a brief second.

"I don't mean to pry, but might I ask what incident from Dean's childhood you're referring to?"

Now, Susan was the one to sound nosy, but she was a psychiatrist. Her occupation covered well for her.

"I'm sorry," Lauren said. "I really shouldn't. It's not my place anymore. I'm sorry to have bothered you."

Lauren thanked them for coming, quickly turned, and walked back into the funeral parlor.

"That was odd," Leah said.

"Very odd," Sidney agreed.

Susan looked at the both of them. "What the hell just happened here?"

Leah was the first to answer. "She said too much. Inadvertently, she revealed more about Dean than she intended."

"The mystery of a dead man thickens," Sidney observed.

Susan stared beyond the front door and into the funeral parlor, debating whether or not to go back inside. No, now was not the right time. She stood perplexed, thinking of only one word.

"Interesting."

———

SILENCE PERVADED THE VAN FOR THE FIRST FIFTEEN minutes of the drive back into Green Valley. Susan sensed the unspoken confoundedness, the loss of words like a bridge between them. Through the quiet, she sat and thought about every moment of her sessions with Dean. Yes, she'd forgotten his mentioning the shadows, but never once had Dean referred to any childhood incident. He'd described his childhood as normal with wonderful, loving parents. Dean's problems had not begun until his adulthood—as far as she knew. Abruptly, Susan broke the maddening silence.

"I'm sorry. I'm still stunned by all this. What childhood incident could Lauren have meant? Dean never mentioned any childhood incident in all the time I treated him."

"Lydia never mentioned a childhood incident either," Leah added.

"This incident," Sidney began. "It has something to do with the paranormal. Why else would she ask if we were paranormal investigators before mentioning it? Obviously, this childhood incident was a family secret of some kind. I know a little something about paranormal incidents and children. Those incidents become secrets, whether they stay with you the rest of your life, or they become buried forever in your subconscious mind."

"Do you think this childhood incident had anything to do with the shadows?" Leah asked.

"No, I don't." Susan remained confident of this. "Remember the video tape? Dean clearly stated that he hadn't seen the shadows until after visiting the abandoned cemetery with Freddy Nash. I suppose there could be many reasons why he wouldn't mention a childhood incident. Maybe it remained so far in the past he felt it was irrelevant."

"He could have also feared not being believed," Sidney said. "After all, we don't know what type of incident occurred."

"There's also the possibility that he blocked it from his mind." Leah referred back to what Sidney mentioned only moments ago. "Children have a way of erasing traumatic things from their recollection."

"But I wonder why Lydia never mentioned it to us." Susan pondered. "Lauren assumed that Lydia contacted us over this childhood occurrence."

"But Lydia didn't know we were paranormal investigators until after we left, remember?" Sidney made an accurate point. Leah added to it.

"What Lydia knew, if anything, may have been limited. Think about it. How much do children know about their parents' childhoods?"

"So, I'm now to assume that some traumatic, paranormal event occurred in Dean Collier's childhood, some disastrous occurrence he may not have even remembered, yet in some way, it shaped who he later became in life."

"That's what it sounds like," Sidney said.

Susan sulked back into the van's plushy passenger seat, wondering just how much she'd failed Dean Collier.

"We'll let some appropriate time pass," she said. "Then, I want to reconnect with Lauren Kessler. She holds the key to the mystery of Dean in more ways than one."

Susan sat speechless, hearing her own words in her mind over again. Something nagged inside her, an inexplicable notion that those words would come back to haunt her.

9

SILENT WATCHERS

THE SPIRIT HAD FLED TO WHERE ITS INFINITE intuition directed. Following its own path, it became swept up in a whirlwind above streets, hills, valleys, and then rivers and skyscrapers. Like the unseen mist that it was, the spirit seeped into the walls of an old, quaint house. The well-preserved house spawned myriad rooms, mostly vacant except for random pieces of stylish furniture: coffee tables, chairs, vases, and velvet sofas.

Caskets set side by side filled another room in which the spirit suddenly wandered. This place, it was a funeral parlor. The spirit found itself here, as if guided by an unseen hand. Lydia was here. This the spirit knew. It gathered its growing strength, its sharpening intuition. The spirit swept through the old house, an angry wind before a turbulent storm. A chair toppled over in its wake. Down solid oak stairs it spiraled until it reached the basement.

Through cloudy vision the spirit had recognized a lounge, a rest room, and a cloak room. But the spirit was drawn to a room on the right, a sterile, green-tiled room where Lydia lay dead on a gurney. White, lifeless, nude beneath a white sheet, she represented an end to the spirit's history. Once, the spirit had sprouted a beautiful flower yet left it behind. Now, that flower had been ruthlessly plucked away, cut short from its bountiful promise. Cold, dead, she slept forever behind closed eyes cast upward into eternity. But the spirit would avenge Lydia, as well as its own senseless and utter removal from this world.

They had not been ready to place Lydia in the casket. She would stay here in this room alone—for now. Here, the spirit lingered. Lydia's body remained, and so had the spirit. This sustained period of time the spirit measured by the equal passing of light and darkness.

Soon, they'd dress her, fix her hair, and then lift her limbs into a portable sling to lower her into the casket. They would treat her gently, lovingly, preparing her for her final rest as if she were a beloved Egyptian princess. They would paint over the grayness of death, a final act to restore her to the beautiful young woman she had been. Lydia would soon appear as if she simply slept.

Light and darkness passed yet again. The spirit hovered above the casket and watched its sleeping beauty. Then, people began to fill the room. The spirit recognized Lydia's husband, his devastation and his pain both blatantly apparent even behind the hardened mask of shock that gripped his face. His parents flanked him on both sides, weeping. But the woman who walked alongside them stirred the spirit into frenzy. It recognized her above all.

Her black hair had tinged with gray. Her shapely, voluptuous form had slouched with the passing of time, but it was her. Removing the dark sunglasses, she revealed how much of her youth had slipped away. Her face had slightly aged, crow's feet and fine lines, but it was a face the spirit remembered well. It was Lauren's.

A few steps behind, a man caught up to Lauren and stood beside her. Large-framed and of a lumberjack build, the man towered above her as he wrapped his arms around her and cradled her to his side. She shed tears into his fine sport jacket. The spirit watched as Lauren then pulled away from him and gazed through teary eyes into the casket.

"She's with her father now," she said to the man. The man, obviously her husband, drew Lauren back toward him and embraced her, calmly shushing her. Lauren's voice lowered slightly, but the spirit heard the hatred, the bitterness in her voice. "He has my baby. From beyond the grave, he's managed to steal her from me. I can *feel it*. Damn him!"

Emotions besieged the spirit: rage, bitterness, hatred, envy. The need for vengeance thrived, as though it were a living pulse. Raw and untamed, it flourished and strengthened the spirit. The spirit felt awakened, cognizant, energized by the notion of revenge. It fed off of it, hosting upon it like a parasite. The spirit witnessed Lauren's pain, her tears. It heard her wails of agony. It felt the slightest vindication from her pain. Vindication—another emotion that seemingly survived beyond physical death. But Lauren's pain was only just beginning.

It remembered how it had once loved her. It remembered bliss that had soured in disappointment, anger that resulted in rage, love that had turned to hate. Her degrading words played over in its memory, forever remaining a part of its existence.

"Look at you. Your life has fallen apart, and you don't even have the strength to put it back together again. You're a loser! I should take my daughter and leave here as fast as possible. I should go somewhere where you'll never be able to poison her life!"

Poison. That was the word she'd used. How ironic. After its exit from this world, Lauren had tried to poison Lydia's mind against Dean, against the person the spirit had been, against the life it had once lived. Now, she would pay. Lauren would feel its malevolent wrath.

The spirit swept through the room, peering down on a multitude of heads as people flooded the funeral parlor. It surveyed them all, most of them crying, sobbing, and expressing shock while uttering the word "tragedy." Then, from a distance, the spirit saw *her* walk through the doorway. Calmly and inconspicuously, Susan and her two cohorts walked over to the poster boards and examined the pictures.

In front of the collage of photos, the spirit lingered beside Susan, watching as her eyes followed a downward, horizontal path. Then, one picture had shaken her to the core. The spirit had not only seen, but somehow felt Susan's reaction to the photo. The photo of Dean, him, holding his daughter had taken her by surprise. The spirit watched her as she frozenly stared at the photo. The spirit sought to send a silent message to her soul. Susan quickly turned and stepped away from the collage of memories.

After paying their respects at the casket, the trio encountered Lydia's husband. Then, as Susan met Lauren for the first time, the spirit hovered slightly above their heads, sensing tension, curiosity, and suspicion between them. The spirit recognized the look in Lauren's eyes. Somewhere deep inside her, she wondered why the woman in front of her was one of the last people to see her daughter alive. Susan's expression revealed her futile attempt to suppress her guilt, her silent remorse. Indeed, it had been her and her associates, who brought the shadows into Lydia's life. Lydia lay dead because of her, and Susan fought hard to redeem herself.

The nervous exchange between them became interrupted. Susan and her friends sought to quickly escape, but Lauren followed them out onto the front terrace. The spirit followed, drifting above them, and then flew out onto the terrace where it might witness an exchange of words. Lauren had cornered Susan about being a paranormal investigator. Then, she lowered her voice as she spoke.

"Did it have anything to do with the incident in Dean's childhood?"

Dean's childhood. The spirit searched through a fog of memories. It felt agitation, anger. The feeling of heat in waves provoked it. What could Lauren have meant? What had she known that the spirit failed to remember? It thought back through its life as Dean. It saw the same familiar images: mother, father, Lauren in a wedding dress, Lydia as a child.

Susan was a liar! Every one of her falsehoods about visiting Lydia ignited the spirit's anger even more. Both Susan and Lauren deserved retribution, and retribution they would receive.

Suddenly, the spirit saw an image of himself as a boy, red hair, and freckles speckling an innocent face. It saw a yellowish-brown haze hovering above the boy. The boy lay in bed, screaming with his head bent back in an upward arch. Then, the suicide memory played over again. A hand raised a pistol to the side of a faceless head. A small explosion erupted. Fire, blood, and then blackness.

Susan and Lauren parted company. The images ceased, but the spirit raged. Its anger multiplied. Its energy soared and strengthened, overturning two patio chairs and causing the puzzled expressions of several onlookers. Glances exchanged. Perhaps it was the sudden wind.

———

HOW FOOLISH SUSAN HAD BEEN TO ASSUME HER doppelganger would find the walls of her stately home impenetrable. How reckless Susan had been to assume she was alone. Silent and unseen, she watched Susan this morning as she sat behind this desk, located a key, and revealed the secret box she kept stashed away. She watched Susan examine the revolver in the light of her desk lamp. Then, Susan quickly returned it to her bottom desk drawer and locked it away. Now, *she* sat behind Susan's desk, solid flesh and bone, appearing just as Susan had before she left with Sidney and Leah.

So, Susan sought to rid her from this world. She welcomed the showdown. Susan seemed to understand the psyche of others, but not her own, yet another of her failures. Drowning in the tension of uncertainty, frightened by the threatening unknown, Susan assumed that pulling the trigger on her doppelganger would be an easy task. Let's see how easy it was for Dr. Logan when the time came. When they met face to face, how easy would it be for Susan to pull the trigger on herself? She'd never fired a gun in her life, outside of that dingy little shooting range.

She remained one step ahead of Susan, and she was going to prove it. She felt underneath the top of the desk for the hidden key. Removing the key from its hideaway, she used it to open the bottom desk drawer. Once she placed the box on the desk, she lifted the cover and looked inside. Yes, this is what Susan would use to end her existence, if she thought it was going to be that easy.

Her plan was simple. She would leave the box here on the desk, and let Susan find it. Then, she thought better of it. Susan would only question whether or not she replaced the box in its original location. She would place the box somewhere where clearly, Susan would realize that someone had removed it from the locked desk drawer.

She took the box and walked into the living room. Then, she set the gray, metal box on the coffee table. When Susan returned from Lydia's viewing and discovered the box, it would send her a clear message. The time to meet her host was drawing near.

She glanced at the clock on the living room wall—a quarter past three. Susan would arrive home soon. She felt her presence coming closer. She watched from the living room's picture window. Soon, Sidney's van pulled into the driveway. Silently, Susan's doppelganger faded back into her ghostly form.

———

SUSAN, SIDNEY, AND LEAH HAD STOPPED FOR AN EARLY dinner on the way home. Now, Susan looked forward to relaxing on the remainder of this quiet Sunday as Sidney's van pulled into her driveway.

"I assure you both, I'll be fine," Susan insisted. "Enjoy the rest of the day. I don't need a babysitter."

She'd been through this several times with Sidney. Now, he

and Leah were making a team effort out of it.

"I just have an odd feeling about leaving you alone," Leah explained.

"Leah, did you see anything else other than this face to face confrontation?" Susan asked.

"No, but I still feel uneasy."

"I'll call you all immediately if I need you, you know that."

Susan whined in persistence, sounding like the world's oldest-living teenager. Sidney and Leah exchanged glances and sighed, as if they were her parents. They made her feel young again, among other things. She exited the van and walked up the driveway. Again, she waved from the front door after punching in the security code.

She watched Sidney slowly pull out of her driveway. She loved all of her team members like they were her children. She laughed to herself at the thought that their love was smothering her; it felt good in an odd way. But she was a big girl. Suddenly, her smile faded. Her face formed a hardened mask at the thought of confronting her doppelganger.

Susan turned away from the front door and walked past the living room without so much as a glance behind her. Upstairs, she changed into her sweats and a bulky shirt, and then returned downstairs to the kitchen. There, she poured herself a glass of wine from the fridge, another reason she wanted to be alone. Taking a seat at her kitchen table, she remembered Leah telling her it was best to keep wine chilled in an ice bucket, that wine lost its flavor in the fridge. Susan thought of all the wine bottles she'd killed decades before Leah was even born. Giggling, she took a long sip from the rounded glass.

A few moments of quiet reflection as the alcohol warmed her blood was just what she needed. She drew another sip from the glass and randomly cast her gaze through her kitchen's bay window. She gazed past her dining room and into the living room. Something gray sat atop the coffee table.

It couldn't be. Her eyes must be deceiving her.

Slowly, she set her glass down on the table and rose from the chair, keeping her gaze upon the faraway object. She retrieved her phone from her purse, which she'd laid on the kitchen counter. Then calmly, she walked into the living room. There it was on the coffee table—the hidden box where she kept her gun.

Susan stood frozen, staring at the box as though what she saw was not real, yet it was. She distinctly remembered locking the box back in the bottom desk drawer before leaving. Someone removed it while she was gone, someone who was here in this house. Instinctively, she pressed the camera function on her phone and snapped a picture of the box on her coffee table. Then, she dialed Leah. Sidney would still be driving.

"What's up?" Leah answered.

"She's here in the house," Susan said. "I can prove it."

Susan continued to stare at the box as she spoke.

"What's wrong?" Leah pressed.

As Susan was about to respond, she felt the drafty chill of someone standing behind her. Slowly and carefully, Susan turned, still clutching the phone in her hand.

"Hello, Susan." Susan's doppelganger stood staring back at her, sporting a strange expression of disappointment.

Susan felt the hair on her head rise. Her heart almost leaped, yet it hadn't. It was herself who stared back at her, yet it was not quite like gazing into a mirror. Her other half appeared opposite, backwards, as though her left were Susan's right, and her right, Susan's left. She was a bizarre reproduction, almost identical in appearance, yet a monstrous enigma.

"So, *there* you are," Susan said placidly.

The other Susan simply shook her head back and forth in a sorrowful expression.

"What's going on?" Leah shouted through the phone.

"It appears I have a guest," Susan replied.

"We're on our way back! Don't hang up!"

Susan eyed the box on the table. She glanced again at the freakish reproduction of herself. Her doppelganger, once a blank slate, now stood like a misshapen child imprinted with her features. She'd been born in a hidden parallel world, the blue realm, a hell filled with opposites.

Susan looked back again at the box on the table.

"Susan!" Leah's voice blared through the phone.

Susan hung up.

10

LAUREN

HER BABY WAS GONE. TOMORROW SHE WOULD SAY goodbye to Lydia forever, not long before they lowered her into the ground. Lauren pondered this as she arrived home from the funeral parlor. She gazed around her modest two-story home, and then at Eugene. He bought this house for her after they were married, and now he and the house were all she had left in this world. These were the last things that were good in her life. Outside of Lydia, they were rectifications of mistakes she'd made in the past. Falling in love way too young, marrying too young, and most of all, marrying Dean. Though she supposed if she hadn't, she wouldn't have had Lydia. But did it matter now? Her baby was gone.

She felt Eugene's hands on her shoulders.

"How about a drink?" he asked. "We could both use one."

Lauren's initial reaction had been to refuse, but why? Did anything matter now?

"Sure," she said. "Make it a double."

Behind their small, living room bar, Eugene poured them both a double of scotch. Lauren sunk down on the couch, kindling her thoughts and memories. Eugene knelt down beside her, handed her the glass, and then placed his hand on her shoulder.

"I have some work to catch up on," he said. "Will you be alright?"

She nodded emphatically. She just wanted to sit and be alone.

"I'll be in my study, if you need me."

He left her alone with years of memories, many of which she'd tried to forget, but there was no forgetting. Painful memories became imprinted forever, like scars that healed but remained faintly visible, especially to the person who bore them. She took a long swig from the glass of scotch and remembered what would never leave her.

How young, wild, and free they'd been in high school. Dean had been an eye-catcher with his rugged, sexy look. She remembered his auburn hair swept off to the side, his sideburns, which were the fashion then, and those green eyes, those damn irresistible eyes he'd passed on to Lydia. She'd been head over heels for him, though she never quite let him know that. It was her way of keeping the upper hand.

Dean had always capitalized on the rough boy appearance, though he hadn't been one, at least not then. She still felt the wind in her hair, the sunshine on her face while riding home on the back seat of his motorcycle after school. Sometimes they'd even ditched classes early and rode to the old railroad tracks, venturing into the woods just beyond, where they went as far as they wanted with each other, each and every time. She remembered their bodies thrashing together, out of sight, beneath the thick forested trees. The feel of him on top of her and inside her, and the scent of her sweet cherry blossom perfume.

Soon, they'd graduated high school, but not before Lauren learned she was pregnant.

It was not a problem for Dean. He would marry her. No child of Dean's would be called illegitimate. Their plan was to marry quickly at City Hall, then tell the world they were expecting. But like most plans, they don't always end as expected. Lauren woke one morning to a sharp pain and a hot stickiness trickling down her legs. She'd gone to the ER, where she miscarried. Through the years, Lauren wondered if that event had been a sign.

She and Dean mourned the loss of a child not meant to be, yet they married anyway. At the insistence of their parents, (his Irish Catholic and hers Protestant) they had a big church wedding, replete with flowers, guests that included family and friends, rice, and a reception. Afterward, they remained two young people in their late-teens, seemingly in love, but now pushed together by circumstances and held to a higher standard they strived desperately to meet.

Dean's uncle procured him a job at the local glass factory. He worked, day in and day out, for many years. Lauren became a housewife, making sure Dean's clothes and work clothes were washed, dried, and folded, and seeing to it that dinner was on the table by five. In addition, she brought in extra income by selling cosmetics door to door. It was a different world then. The quaint, humble scenario was expected of her, of both of them. They smiled and conformed, yet something between them remained unspoken.

Years into their marriage, she noticed how Dean appeared lost at times. Sometimes he would suddenly go quiet, his eyes listlessly gazing into somewhere, as if he were trying to remember something. As time went on, Lauren noticed fits of agitation and a sudden spark of temper she'd never seen before. Then, he would appear calm, as if nothing happened.

Tension grew between them. Lauren assumed it was because she failed to conceive again after her miscarriage. They'd both wanted another baby, yet years passed, and each time she thought she was pregnant turned out to be a false alarm. Then one day, twelve years after her miscarriage, Lauren learned she was expecting another child.

Lydia would become their pride and joy and their only child. She was a sweet, adorable little girl with bright green eyes peeping innocently above soft bubbly cheeks. Lauren recalled how attached Lydia was to her father; how she stood clutching Dean's leg with one hand and grasping her blanket and teddy bear with the other. Lydia had been Daddy's little girl, so much so that Lauren felt somewhat thwarted. Now, Lauren felt the pain twist in her chest like a knife, knowing her daughter's story had ended tragically, just like her father's.

As Lydia grew older, Dean's erratic behavior progressed. Their fights grew louder and more intense. Soon, Lydia would witness it all. Lauren had continued to wonder about the silent spells Dean appeared to fall under. Those reveries occurred just before the change in his behavior. Dean had been a moderate drinker. Lauren knew that alcohol was not his problem, though it hadn't helped. Yet something was there in the dark recesses of Dean's mind, something in his past that he failed to remember.

Lauren decided to ask his parents. Doris and Henry Collier were meek, gentle people, yet underneath it all they lingered in the traditional art of discretion, and often, denial. She'd wondered how much they would even remember, let alone admit. One Sunday, she, Dean, and Lydia paid them a visit. Lauren convinced Dean to take Lydia down the street to the neighborhood park. When he agreed, Lauren was left alone with Dean's parents.

"I'm worried about him," she told them. "It's like he's trying to remember something but can't. Then afterward, I don't recognize him. As time goes by, it's getting worse. He won't talk to me. He becomes irritated and angry with me."

She noticed Doris' eyes shift toward her husband and then down to her lap. Henry, also keeping his eyes down, sighed in what sounded like defeat and frustration. They knew exactly what Lauren was talking about; they'd seen it before.

"What? What is it you're not telling me?" Lauren insisted. "What is Dean trying to remember?" Doris and Henry exchanged nervous glances. "You need to tell me before they get back. I don't want whatever this thing is to affect Lydia."

Doris looked to her husband. Fear stricken by a prospect she hadn't considered before, she skeptically contemplated her answer.

Henry glanced back at her, silently conveying the inevitability of the truth. Doris returned her gaze to Lauren.

"When Dean was a little boy, he became violently ill," she began. "At least, that's what we thought. At first, he seemed quiet, distant, and then I realized he had a fever. Not long after the fever broke, it would return, spiking to a temperature higher than before. I kept him home from school for a few days and called the doctor. That was back when they made house calls. The doctor diagnosed it as nothing more than the common flu and prescribed an antibiotic. Dean showed no signs of chicken pox, mono, strep, or any other serious infection. We assumed he'd be okay."

"At first, he seemed to perk up a little." Henry picked up where Doris left off. "Then, we awoke one night to our ten-year-old boy screaming. When we got to his room, we found him thrashing around in bed, his head arched backward, and screaming like he was on fire. And that's exactly what it looked like. His skin was scorching red, and hot to the touch. Sweat soaked his hair. It took all the strength we had to restrain him." Henry paused and swallowed hard. "Then, when he spoke, his voice was different. The voice was not our boy's."

Doris took a deep breath and shuddered from the painful memory. "He cursed at us. We never used words like that at home, and I'm almost positive he didn't hear them at school, not at that time." Tears welled in her eyes. She lifted her hand, a simple physical plea silently asking why. "This spell our son had fallen under, it went on for a week."

The sobs broke from her. Tears burst through a dam that had been built up for years. Henry wrapped his arm around his wife's shoulder and spoke for her.

"We called a priest. We didn't know what else to do. Given what we saw and experienced, no doctor could've helped our son. A psychiatrist was out of the question."

"They would have taken our boy and committed him." Doris' tone became adamant, defensive. "We knew he wasn't crazy. Whatever was wrong with him occurred suddenly, as if—as if something had gotten a hold of our son and was trying to take him away from us."

Doris continued to sob. Henry patted her shoulder.

"The priest was someone we knew socially," Henry explained. "He was a young priest, relocated here from Massachusetts and landed a position in the church we attended. Whispers and rumors swept the town about how this young priest, this Father Maguire, was either blessed or cursed with experience in exorcism and battling the occult. No one knew how true any of it was. Regardless of what was true and what wasn't, I called him, and he came."

Lauren remembered the shock she felt listening to the story. She'd sat stunned, unable to conceive what she was hearing. Doris and Henry were good, honest people. She saw the pain, the horror, and the shame this childhood occurrence caused them just being reminded of it. She never doubted their sincerity for a moment.

"Wait a minute," she said. "You mean to tell me that Dean was *possessed?*"

Doris and Henry met her skepticism with solid, resolute expressions.

"Father Maguire had no reservations at all, whatsoever," Doris said. "He took one look at Dean in the bed, and it was almost like he knew."

"He performed an exorcism." Henry's revelation sounded like a confession. Silence ensued. Lauren heard her heartbeat through the quiet. "When our boy began cursing us and God, we knew what it was. The vile, defiant, blasphemy we heard coming from that thing in the bed would never have come from our boy."

Lauren listened to the story of how Dean, a boy whose soul had been taken captive by some type of malevolence, writhed in bed, kicking, screaming, and foaming at the mouth. Within hours, Father Maguire had driven the dark force from the boy who was left whimpering, crying, and hanging from the edge of the bed. Lauren felt a painful knot form in her Adam's apple, thinking of the trauma her husband experienced as a boy. When Lauren referred to the experience as demonic, Henry clarified.

"Father Maguire was not so convinced that what possessed Dean was a demon. He claimed that many types of malevolent forces existed, and that demons were more difficult to defeat. He confided to us that he once witnessed an exorcism involving a demon that lasted for days. Whatever it was that inhabited our son hadn't lasted long against the young priest. We are forever in his debt."

"When it was over, Dean had no idea what occurred." Doris regained her composure. "To this day, he has never remembered. Better that it stays that way."

Henry continued, not overstating the obvious. "Later, Father Maguire relocated to a church not far from here. He makes a point of calling us every Christmas and asking about Dean. Dean only remembers him as the priest who prayed for him when he was deathly ill. We never spoke of the event again."

Moments later, Dean and Lydia returned from the park. When Dean saw his wife and parents huddled so seriously together, he asked. "Everything alright in here?"

Lauren recalled her speechlessness, her muffled attempt at a response, and then Henry coming to her rescue.

"Everything's fine, son. Have a nice time in the park?"

Dean's suspicions were never roused. He never learned the extent of their conversation. Years passed without Lauren ever mentioning Dean's childhood secret. She would never have betrayed Doris and Henry's trust. Besides, her main concern had been Lydia. Lauren knew Dean had no recollection of this childhood event, yet she continued to watch him. After all, forgotten childhood memories had a way of recurring, didn't they? From then on, she paid attention to the change in him when his moods fluctuated. She listened carefully to his words when he became angry. None of it seemed outside of the emotional issues Dean silently struggled with from time to time. But eventually, Dean's behavior worsened.

His mood swings ranged from cheer to outrage within minutes. Lauren and Dean fought as the bills grew heftier, and the household income remained the same. Each month, they struggled to financially stay afloat. Lauren continued to feel thwarted as Dean became parent number one, and she assumed the identity of parent number two.

Then, Dean lost his job at the glass factory. Regardless of the stable economy that existed at that time, supply for the local glass factory far outweighed demand. Like many Pittsburgh industries before it, it folded. Dean became one of many workers laid off, yet automatically entitled to unemployment compensation. As Dean collected unemployment that paid just sufficiently under his normal take-home pay, his drinking increased.

Lauren had nagged him to find another job, yet admittedly, there was nothing. Dean had no college education, no formal trade, just the job his uncle acquired for him after high school. In a changing, pre-technological world, Dean found himself unwanted, unneeded, and severely under qualified. Sometimes for hours, he'd sit quietly. Lauren wondered how far into the past his mind was wandering. In order to keep Dean's childhood secret buried, to shield Lydia from it, and to protect Doris and Henry, Lauren had broken his silent spells with her persistent nagging.

That's when he exploded.

He'd beaten her with his fists, something he'd never done before. Something about him that day was not the Dean she'd always known, the Dean she'd fallen in love with when she was just a teenager. Something changed him. He'd pulled her up from the floor by her hair and continued to pummel her. He'd broken her nose, blackening both of her eyes. Lydia stood upstairs, listening the whole time. Even now, Lauren suspected Lydia witnessed some, if not all of the attack. But now, she would never know for sure.

After she called 911, the cops had taken Dean away in handcuffs. She had him arrested, but then she thought of Henry and Doris, and of course, Lydia. She decided not to press charges if

Dean agreed to be committed into the Meadowbrook Mental Facility, not far outside of Green Valley. He agreed, yet Dean was never the same afterward. They remained separated, but when she saw Dean, he seemed afraid, paranoid, and possibly delusional. She often wondered if the stay in Meadowbrook had made his situation even worse.

Not long after, Dean pointed a pistol at his temple and pulled the trigger. For years, Lydia blamed Lauren for her father's suicide.

Then, there was Susan Logan, the woman who attended Lydia's viewing. Susan Logan had mysteriously shown up at Lydia's house shortly before she'd fallen to her death. Lydia had researched Susan on the internet and discovered she was a paranormal investigator. After learning these facts, Lauren became convinced she'd heard that name before—Susan Logan. Lauren remained almost certain that Dean's psychiatrist at Meadowbrook had been a woman with the same name. In their brief conversation today, Susan mentioned that she was a psychiatrist, and that she was a *friend* of Dean's. Susan Logan had looked her straight in the face and never mentioned that she was in fact, Dean's psychiatrist —why?

Knowing Susan and her friends were paranormal investigators, Lauren felt sure Lydia had consulted them about Dean's childhood secret. Lauren shared this information with her daughter once Dean was gone, and both Doris and Henry had passed. But when Lauren discreetly asked, Susan had appeared off guard. Her puzzled expression told Lauren that Susan had no idea what she was talking about, which thickened the mystery surrounding her.

Lydia hadn't contacted paranormal investigators. So, what had Susan Logan *really* wanted with Lydia? Why did Lydia mysteriously and tragically lose her life only hours later? Lauren took another swig of her scotch. She would wait until after the funeral tomorrow. Then, she would find out just what Susan Logan and her team were hiding.

She closed her eyes and tried to let the myriad thoughts that overwhelmed her slip away. She sipped the scotch this time, focusing only on the cool burn as it slid down her throat and the warm sensation as it coursed through her veins. She would feel more relaxed after a hot bath. Lauren set her glass down on the coffee table and rose from the couch.

She'd taken only a few steps and then stopped. Something took hold of her, and it wasn't the scotch. She felt an incredible weight anchoring her down, a pressure as if gravity had suddenly multiplied. Her eyesight blurred. She stared up at the ceiling lights as the world grew fuzzy and distorted.

Then, she felt a great detachment, like she'd been yanked away from her own body. Lauren became suddenly lost in an eerie dual existence she couldn't fathom. She could see her own body struggling to hoist one heavy leg after another. She was here, and she was *there*. Lauren was no longer in control. A sea of darkness enveloped her, drowning her deeper and deeper into a state of confusion.

———

ENRAPT IN THE THRALL OF VENGEANCE, THE SPIRIT attached itself to Lauren. It immersed itself in her familiarity: her face, the sound of her voice, the smell of her perfume. Her mere essence provoked a barrage of images, memories, and feelings that flourished too fast for the spirit to catch, but it understood. While the spirit felt a tinge of love, it also felt hurt, rage, and betrayal. The spirit had surrounded Lauren on the veranda of the funeral parlor, never losing sight of its mission—to possess her, consume her, and to ultimately destroy her.

It remained with her in the car on the way home. It watched her project love to another man, a man she now called her husband. A love it had once known. The spirit watched as she sat on the couch, drowning her miseries in alcohol. It knew her every silent thought. It saw the images that played out in her mind.

The images of young love caused the spirit a pang of bitter heartbreak. It witnessed the love, the struggles, and the uncertainty all over again, yet from Lauren's perspective. Then, it saw *their* faces—mother and father. The spirit heard the sound of their long lost voices. Then, it stole their words from the recesses of Lauren's mind and from the depths of her soul.

"The priest was someone we knew socially."

"He performed an exorcism."

The spirit heard the word over and over.

"Exorcism...Exorcism...Exorcism..."

"When it was over, Dean had no idea what occurred." Mother's voice. *"To this day, he has never remembered. Better that it stays that way."*

"Dean only remembers him as the priest who prayed for him when he was deathly ill."

Mother and Father's voices prompted more images, images of a forgotten childhood. The spirit saw himself as a child, writhing in bed, screaming up to a silent Heaven. A young priest initiated the sign of the cross, a purple alb draped around his shoulders. The priest's voice started low, and then boomed. The boy's soul squirmed and struggled. The spirit felt itself thrashing along with the boy. Then, the images ceased. The voices stopped. Memories vanished.

Enraged, the spirit sought to see more. It had invaded Lauren's mind and read her memories, and by doing so, subjected itself to the rudest of awakenings. The images of the boy and the priest were familiar, but now, those images lingered far away in a distant past the spirit failed to pinpoint. Confusion fueled its anger.

Lauren sipped the glass, and then rose from the couch. A secret, she kept a secret hidden in her mind and soul, one about the boy and the priest. The spirit needed to see more. It needed to know. It needed inside her.

It felt the heat of her humanly flesh as it neared her. Her heartbeat pounded like the repetitive beat of a drum. Closer, the spirit sensed her life force, a free flow of energy that seemed endless. Gathering the strength it had mustered through time, the spirit dared itself to extinguish that life force, to silence that pulse that continued unfairly. Her heat intensified as the spirit enwrapped itself in her flesh, an unseen python gripping its unsuspecting prey.

Then, it slipped inside her.

It felt the warmth of her blood wrap around its bodiless form like a blanket. It saw her beating heart in a fast flash of vision. Suddenly, with her eyes, it looked up at the ceiling lights. Blurriness as it gazed through the eyes of another, yet the distortion was temporary. The harder Lauren fought to gain control, the more she slipped away from her body, like a bad swimmer failing to grasp a lifeboat in a darkened sea.

As Lauren lost control, the spirit's sight became clearer and sharper. Yet human movement had been long forgotten. The malevolent spirit invading Lauren's body moved slowly, dragging one foot in front of the other from the profound weight of human legs. It inched forward, step by infantile step, feeling the plush white carpeting beneath bare human feet.

Hijacked human eyes absorbed the surroundings. The white brick walls matched the carpeting and framed a fireplace on one end. Lauren's body lumbered to the mantle above it. A framed wedding picture of Lauren and her husband sat atop it. She smiled in the picture, happier than she'd been before.

The spirit turned away from the mantle. In its new human form, it trudged down a long hallway that led to the rooms of the upper floor. A light shined from the hallway ceiling, illuminating modern artwork that adorned the walls. A repetitive clicking noise sounded from behind a closed door on the left at the end of the hallway. Outside the door, a wooden cabinet with double glass doors stood erect and facing out where the hallway ended.

The spirit gained greater and quicker movement the longer it inhabited Lauren's body. It made it to the end of the hallway, where it stood and observed its reflection in the cabinet's glass doors. The likeness was Lauren's, a stark reflection of a human possessed. Bloodshot eyes, irises that appeared almost violet from a sudden change in hue.

But what was artfully and skillfully positioned behind the glass doors lured and then captured the spirit's greater attention. The spirit looked closely with Lauren's eyes. Long, narrow steel barrels extended from wooden handles. The long objects stood aligned side by side. The spirit shifted Lauren's eyes downward. It recognized something—a trigger. Rifles, the objects were rifles. The misty fog that engrossed the spirit dissipated with each passing moment it spent anchored in its host. As the physical world became clearer, the spirit recognized what it beheld—a gun cabinet. Beneath the larger portion of the cabinet was a smaller glass door, one that housed two shelves stacked atop each other. The spirit recognized the smaller guns stored on the shelves—a pistol, and a revolver.

The suicide memory played over again. A hand raised a pistol, and a finger pulled the trigger. Fire, blood, and then life faded to black. Even as it inhabited the flesh of its host, the spirit retained its own memories. Now, the suicide memory appeared more vividly. The details grew sharper, as if the spirit gained greater power of memory from its host.

The clicking noise emanating from the room on the left continued. Typing, the spirit remembered the sound of typing. Gazing down at the lower cabinet, it knew what must be done. It bent down and tried to open the cabinet—locked. Quickly and resolutely, the spirit drew one heavy fist back and plunged it crashing through the lower glass case. Glass shattered. The typing stopped.

Maneuvering Lauren's hand, it pulled the pistol off the shelf and through the broken shards. Gun in bloody hand, it shuffled Lauren's feet toward the door. It gripped the door handle and turned it quickly. Eugene stood behind the door, a horrified expression on his face: shock, disbelief, confusion.

Lauren's breathing grew rapid; her heart pounded. Eugene reached his hand out.

"Lauren, honey, what's going on? Your eyes—"

The spirit raised Lauren's arm, aimed, and pulled the trigger. A small explosion erupted, the sound like a loud firecracker. A red blotch widened over Eugene's shirt, in the middle of his chest, the bullet piercing his heart. Eugene stumbled backward and tumbled to the floor, his abandoned laptop up and running.

But the spirit knew it could not inhabit this body forever. It wouldn't last. Images of the suicide memory appeared over and over. The pain of that moment belonged to Lauren as much as it had Dean. Given this truth, one last thing remained. The spirit raised the pistol up to Lauren's head. Then, using her finger, it squeezed the trigger.

Fire, blood, and then life faded to black—all over again.

11

FACE TO FACE

"SHE'S INSIDE THE HOUSE WITH HER!" LEAH SHOUTED. "Turn around and go back!"

Sidney and Leah had not yet exited the spiraling mazes of King's Haven. The drive through the lofty residential area usually took more than five minutes, but today, Sidney had taken his time. Now, he slammed hard on the van's brakes, screeching to a halt merely feet from the gated entrance. He shifted the van into reverse, pulled into a nearby driveway, and then quickly turned in the opposite direction, back to where they'd just reluctantly left.

"I knew we shouldn't have left her," Sidney exclaimed. "Tahoe mentioned the possibility of this doppelganger invading the house, and we let her stay there alone!"

Leah had already redialed Susan and sat impatiently waiting for an answer. "Damn it, Susan! She's not picking up."

"No, because she's planning to handle this on her own. I think the good doctor Logan has as of late, secretly lost it. She wants to destroy her once and for all—most likely right after she psychoanalyzes her."

Sidney's odd sense of humor remained ever present, indicating the nervousness he felt in this moment, but Leah admitted he had a point.

"Let's hope that gives us some extra time," she said. "I'm calling Dylan and Brett and telling them to meet us at Susan's house."

Sidney lead footed the gas pedal. The van barreled back through the winding streets of King's Haven, the accelerator purring louder and louder. Leah's heart pounded as Dylan's phone continued to ring.

————

"SO, THERE ARE NO WALLS THAT WILL STOP YOU." SUSAN stood face to face with her doppelganger, just as Tahoe had predicted. Remaining calm, she stared at her ghastly clone, noticing her identical features while honing in on her lopsided symmetry. Susan stood waiting for an answer, her heart pounding. She watched a puzzled expression form on a face that belonged to her. Then as the doppelganger spoke again, Susan realized that even her voice was the same.

"Our thoughts are the same also," she said. "Yet I can't quite fathom how you learned nothing from Taryn and Angus. They also moved through walls, didn't they?"

"Yes, but that little fact seemed to slip my mind after everything I'd been through, being left behind in the blue realm while you gave your flawed performance as me," Susan retorted, her voice climbing slightly. "Besides, I never believed it would happen this way, especially since you made a life of your own with my name and identity, not to mention my credit cards. I thought you'd remain free in the world and live out your existence on my money."

She laughed lightly. Susan felt the stun of it, watching her imitate her own slight chuckle to perfection, yet it was no imitation, it was natural. They stood feet apart from each other, both of them apprehensive to sit while the other stood. Susan's phone rang repeatedly.

"You might want to get that," the doppelganger advised. "It's Leah. She and Sidney are on their way back here, and when you don't answer, Leah will call in the rest of the team."

"Let her," Susan said. "But first, you and I have unfinished business."

Susan's phone stopped ringing.

The doppelganger waltzed a few steps to the right and plopped down on one of the living room chairs. She extended her hand, inviting Susan to do the same.

"Take a seat, Susan," she said. "Trust me, I'm not going to reach inside that box, grab the gun, and end *your* life. I wouldn't do that to you. I'd be ending my own existence as well."

Susan stood erect, trembling slightly.

"And what's to stop me from reaching inside that box and ending this all right now?"

"You could, Susan," she said. "But you won't. There's too much you want to know, too much you want to discover from me." Her identical face formed a familiar and sober expression. "Besides, the members of your team already believe their beloved Dr. Logan has 'lost it,' as Sidney aptly put it. It wouldn't be wise of you, not while they're on their way here."

Susan took a deep, quivering breath and stepped cautiously to the edge of the couch, directly adjacent to where her double sat fixedly. They remained far away enough for sufficient space, yet close enough to talk face to face. The box on the coffee table caught the corner of Susan's eye. Susan was not yet ready to discard the option of reaching over and ending the other's monstrous existence, but she quickly ditched the idea from her mind, remembering that their thoughts were one.

"You lured me into the Black Mirror," Susan began, her tone blunt and accusing. "You convinced me that I would solve its mystery, all the while your likeness cast a spell over me. You drew me in so Angus could free himself, and of course, you would live *my* life." Susan paused. "And you almost got away with it. You tried to impersonate me, yet you weren't good enough. Since then, you've bilked me out of thousands of dollars and counting. So, tell me, am I supposed to welcome you? Turn my life over to you? Is that what you expect?"

"I expect nothing from you, Susan," she said, her expression shaping into a plea for sympathy. "I want nothing other than the chance to remain free, or to even coexist with you if such a thing would be possible." Another pause ensued. "The world is a big enough place, Susan. You and I could even take on this big, brazen world together."

Susan simply stared at her, her mind attempting to process the rabid thoughts of her bizarre counterpart. Susan leaned forward.

"You're insane," she declared.

"No more insane than you, Dr. Logan."

The doppelganger shifted her eyes toward the box on the table. Susan followed her meaning with her own eyes. Her point was easily understood. Dr. Susan Logan, highly esteemed psychiatrist, the same shrink who once misdiagnosed Dean Collier, had freely and quickly thought to end this debacle with a gun, knowing she would get away with it. No corpse would have been left to identify. Susan suddenly felt as if something in her mind had been unlocked. She felt the showering of realizations, truth, and clarity, but the weight of her guilt and her embarrassment became an invisible monolith bearing down upon her.

Keeping her eyes on the box, Susan sprang from the couch, and then stood frozen. She glanced over at her sinister double, whose smug expression taunted her. She knew damn well Susan wouldn't do it. An egregious act such as striking down her own semblance would never leave her as long as she lived. Not even the great Dr. Logan would rise beyond such a trauma.

Instinctively, Susan turned her head away, distracted by an approaching sound. Brakes screeched as Sidney's van came to an abrupt halt in front of the house. Susan watched through the picture window's white curtain. The van's usual purring now sounded like a roar.

"Well, well," the other Susan exclaimed. "Sidney and Leah are back—just in time."

———

SIDNEY REELED FROM THE BITTER STING OF SELF-reproach. Anger seized him like his white-knuckled grip on the steering wheel. Leah did not reproach him for transferring his anger to the gas pedal. His screeching halt landed squarely in front of Susan's house.

"I walked with her into the house time and time again," Sidney lamented. "I could feel something wasn't right. I kept letting her shoo me away."

"There's no sense in beating yourself up, Sid," Leah said. "You couldn't have known if Susan's doppelganger was inside the house. We're not dealing with a regular human being."

"She's been inside the house the whole time, the *whole goddamn time!* We should have intervened, all of us, especially after Tahoe warned us of this possibility. We should have camped inside the house and smoked the bitch out!"

"And you know Susan would've never let that happen. Come on, let's get inside."

As Leah opened the van's passenger door, her phone rang. It was Dylan. She pressed a button on her phone and quickly answered.

"Dylan, Sid and I are at Susan's. You need to get here quickly. The doppelganger is inside the house with Susan."

"I'm on my way," Dylan replied through the speakerphone. "I'll call Brett and Tahoe."

Sidney could hear the faraway sound of Dylan's voice as he stomped up the stone stairs leading to Susan's front porch. Leah ran to catch up to him, but Sidney already stood on the porch, pounding the front door with his fists.

———

ENDING IT WAS NO LONGER AN OPTION. SIDNEY'S FISTS barraged her front door.

"Susan, open the door, now!"

Susan heard the anger in Sidney's voice, the temper that often reared its ugly head to replace the embarrassment of one's own fear. His rapid pounding continued.

"You'd better get that," the doppelganger said. "It sounds like Leah won't be able to stop him from busting the door down."

Susan hesitated. "Do you see what you're causing?"

The other Susan lifted her left eyebrow, a facial expression Susan sometimes exhibited unconsciously.

"Let them in," she advised. "After all, we're already acquainted."

"Susan!" Sidney pounded harder and louder this time.

"Susan? Let us in." Leah shouted through the door, her voice muffled, yet clearly audible. "Don't do anything you'll regret. You know that we, as a society, need to speak with her. You're right, this needs to end, but you need to think objectively."

"It sounds like Miss Leeds had become quite the psychologist," the doppelganger observed. "Let's hope she doesn't lose it like her mentor."

Her sarcastic tone sounded so familiar. Susan leered sharply at her, only to be met with her own wry smile.

"Alright," Susan agreed. "But remember, you brought this on yourself."

Susan back stepped and walked sideways to the door, never taking her eyes off of her mischievous double. She tapped her four-digit code into the security system, then after a beep and a click, she opened the front door. Sidney lurked with his arm crooked against the door frame. Leah stood behind him on her tiptoes, peeping inside over his shoulder.

Motioning with her head sideways, Susan signaled them to

come inside. Stepping through the doorway, Sidney glared at the doppelganger still seated in the chair.

"Please, come in both of you." Susan's doppelganger opened her hands in a welcoming gesture. She sat smugly, self-confident, and seemingly self-assured that the spacious house was equally hers. "Long time no see, as they say." She pointed to the box on the coffee table. "Take a look at what you've stopped, Sidney. You know, you're right about her. She's lost it."

Sidney walked over to the box on the coffee table, never removing his eyes from her. Then, he looked into the box, and then at Susan.

"Where did you get that?" He pointed inside the box. "Is she right? Have you lost it?"

Susan ignored the question and motioned him toward the couch. "You both think we should learn from her, and discover her secrets? Now is your chance." She turned and closed the front door.

Sidney and Leah stepped slowly to the three-piece sectional couch and sat next to each other, their eyes never leaving the doppelganger seated in the chair so close to them. For just a moment, Leah looked away from her, turning her attention to Susan.

"Dylan is on his way here," she said. "I believe Brett and Tahoe are also."

"Wonderful!" the doppelganger exclaimed. "It'll be so nice to get reacquainted and conduct the meeting we never had a chance to have."

Leah slowly turned her head once again in the doppelganger's direction. "Did you really think you'd be able to pull it off? Infiltrating our meeting as Susan, and thinking we wouldn't know her well enough to know something was seriously off? Did you think I wouldn't see through you?"

"That was my fault," she said. "I should have known I could never fool the likes of you, Leah Leeds, not with your powerful sight that Angus had warned me about."

"Angus Marlowe was an evil man," Leah responded. "And you were his accomplice. You both almost stole Susan's life away. Then, there's Taryn Page. Madison Page will never be the same again, all because of you and Angus Marlowe. And you think Sidney and I should stop Susan from ending your existence? Why?"

The doppelganger laughed, much like Susan. "That *is* why you're here, isn't it?"

"You're an arrogant bitch, you know that?" Sidney nearly sprung from the couch. "To tell you the truth, I don't need answers that badly. Yes, we're paranormal investigators, but all protocols tell us safety first, so I don't mind if she wastes you. As far as I'm concerned, none us will have witnessed a damn thing."

"Take it easy, Sid." Leah grabbed onto his shirt. "Don't let her get the best of you."

Sidney turned his gaze away from her, looked back at Susan, and then back at the doppelganger, finally realizing that they wore the same clothes.

"Amazing," he said. "You've copied her down to the final detail." He turned back to Susan. "Susan, stay on that side of the room, in case she tries to pull a fast one on us."

"*That* won't happen," Leah snapped. "Besides, there's that one little thing you haven't been able to master." Leah turned her full attention to the doppelganger. "The walk, that's something you need to tell us about—why you can't seem to balance with normal, human equilibrium."

The three of them watched the other Susan's smug smile fade into a lost and empty expression.

"Look closely, Sid," Leah continued. "You can see her features are reversed, like they would be if one looked into a mirror."

Sidney removed his glasses and crooked his head closer in the doppelganger's direction. "Yes, I see that. Why don't you begin by telling us why that is?"

"Because she was born in a world of opposites, isn't that correct?" Susan spoke as she stepped closer to the couch. "The blue realm was an alternate realm filled with opposites, a strange hell sporting parallel entities of everything, including humans. As a result, in this world, she continues to carry that particular curse. She's Susan Logan in appearance, thoughts, voice, and even wardrobe. Everything except for the fact that my right is her left and so forth, which makes her nothing more than a sad, unbalanced reproduction."

Sidney and Leah watched as two sets of the same eyes became locked in a gripping, silent showdown. Susan could sense their nervous tension as they observed her, and then *her*. Susan's heart pounded harder and faster, knowing that her doppelganger knew her thoughts right now. She knew Susan wanted to quickly reach inside the box and end her existence before Sidney and Leah could do anything about it.

But what if her doppelganger also suddenly felt the urge to end it all? What if she decided she no longer wanted to live, especially after her blatant flaws had been so sharply pointed out? What would stop *her* from reaching for the gun in the box and ending Susan's life, and consequently her own? If she realized there was no real life ahead for her, she could end it but take Susan with her first. What if she hurt Sidney and Leah in the process?

Now, the urge to kill her became uncontrollable.

"Sit down, Susan." Her double's tone sounded strict, almost in command. Their eyes remained locked together in a threatening exchange. "You'll never be able to explain the sound of the gunshot. Then, what's his name—Detective Goddard—will arrive so fast you'll never have time to get your stories straight."

Susan felt the sudden sting affixed to her words. The doppelganger leaned forward in her chair, waiting for Susan's reaction.

"That's right," she continued. "We should all talk about Detective Goddard—him—and a few other things once everyone arrives."

The doppelganger's left eyebrow cocked in an upward arch. Susan's heart nearly stopped.

12

THE BURGEONING PRESENT

TAHOE SAT ENVISIONING THE BURGEONING PRESENT. The vision abruptly overcame him as the waitress asked if he and Brett had found everything satisfactory. As the waitress cleared the table and turned away, Tahoe closed his eyes and glimpsed the scene, as if it played on a distant screen. One Susan sat in a chair; the other Susan stood in the center of the room. He saw Sidney nearly eject himself from the couch, Leah grasping onto his shirt. Lately, Tahoe's visions seemed more profound, more real in their depictions, and this one was no different.

"Are you okay?" Brett's hand reached over and clasped his shoulder.

Tahoe opened his eyes.

"It's happening, my friend. Susan's confrontation with her doppelganger is taking place as we speak. Sidney and Leah are there."

"Come on, let's go. We're only ten minutes from King's Haven."

Brett stood, retrieved his wallet from his back pocket, and paid the check on the way out. Within minutes, they were in Brett's car and back out on the road. Brett headed in the direction of King's

Haven, pumping the gas pedal and cruising just below the speed limit.

"I'm apprehensive, yet anxious to meet this being," Tahoe said. "I wonder if she is the key to what I've been seeing, the discolored haze that hovered over Susan in my visions, but I doubt this."

"Then we need to find out, right away." Brett checked his phone as he slowed and stopped at a red light. "I wonder why no one's called me yet."

Brett lived a considerable distance away from the rest of the team, but luckily, today he and Tahoe decided to travel into the city for dinner. As they waited for the light to turn green, Brett's phone rang.

"It's Dylan."

"Answer him," Tahoe advised. "Things are about to begin, my friend."

———

AFTER LEAH'S CALL, DYLAN GOT INTO HIS CAR AND peeled through the front gate of his estate. Cited for speeding twice in the past six months, he slowed upon arriving at an intersection where a red light halted him and three cars in front of him. Paused in traffic, he realized something as he noticed the EVP recorder lying on the front passenger seat. Luckily, he'd forgotten to bring it back inside the house. Now, it was the only piece of tech equipment with him because before dashing out of the house, he hadn't taken the time to gather any gear, not his infrared cameras, not even a video camera. Yet Brett was in charge of the team's tech apparatus.

Brett—he'd forgotten to call Brett. He quickly chose Brett's number from his call list just as the light turned green. Dylan steered with one hand, phone in the other, consciously monitoring his speed until he reached a certain point where the coast was clear. When Brett answered, Dylan spoke rapidly, telling him about the call from Leah.

"The doppelganger is inside the house with Susan," he said. "She must've been hiding there the whole time. Sidney and Leah have gone back to the house."

"I know," Brett said. "Tahoe saw it happening in a vision. We're on our way there now."

"So, I take it your video camera is back at your house?"

"Shit!" Brett exclaimed. "Yes, it is, but Sidney always has one of everything inside the van. I'm sure of it."

"If not, we'll have to rely on our camera phones."

"That shouldn't be a problem," Brett assured him. "Technically, any type of documentation for our archives will be sufficient, just as long as it can be considered proof."

"We're all about to meet our director's doppelganger face to face. I don't see how much more proof we need. We all have cameras on our phones. I also have the EVP recorder with me. I want to know if she's the voice on the recording from the cemetery."

"Tahoe agrees," Brett said. "If it's not the doppelganger's voice, and if she's not responsible for the haze Tahoe's been seeing in his visions, then we may have another problem on our hands. We need to figure out what's happening."

Then, Brett revealed his exact location, pointing out that he was five minutes away from King's Haven.

"I'm almost that close," Dylan said. "I'll see you there."

Dylan turned his head in all directions, not spotting any discreet checkpoints along the roadside. He floored the pedal yet remained watchful as his speedometer inched past sixty miles per hour. If there was any occasion when his speeding was warranted, this was one of them. Dylan felt a strange sensation, as if all the dark forces of the hidden world were suddenly coming together.

13

EXTORTION

Her words stunned the three of them into silence. Now, *she* had control of the room. Wide-eyed, blindsided, and subdued, Susan, Sidney, and Leah stared at her. In speechless apprehension, they waited for her to continue.

"We all know that Dylan, Brett, and the seer—what's his name, Tahoe—are on their way here. With respect to the rest of the team, I think it's best to wait until they arrive. What I have to say needs to be heard by everyone."

Still seated in the chair adjacent to Susan's three-piece sectional, the doppelganger maintained a clear-cut view of the driveway as she sat facing the picture window. After observing how her words had caused their sudden and undivided attention, she became distracted by a black Camaro as it pulled in front of the driveway.

"Mr. Taylor and his guest have arrived," she announced. Susan, Sidney, and Leah turned their attentions toward the picture window. Looking out, they noticed another car pull behind Brett's. Dylan had also arrived. "And Mr. Rasche makes a full house —perfect!"

Silent tension lingered throughout the room like a thick fog.

All eyes watched through the picture window, silent efforts to escape the impending explosion. As Brett, Tahoe, and Dylan stepped up onto the porch, Susan walked over to the front door to admit her guests. As they stepped through the door, Brett and Dylan held their phones in front of them, recording Susan's nearly identical subject sitting smugly in the chair.

"Boys, boys," she said. "You might want to turn the cameras off for what I'm about to say, but that's entirely up to you. I think additional records of your misdeeds won't be necessary, do you?"

Not entirely understanding, Brett and Dylan lowered their phones as Susan held up her hands in a plea.

"Let's see what she has to say first," she said.

Behind the younger men, Tahoe stood watching her, examining every line, wrinkle, and familiar feature of her face. The doppelganger craned her head a little to the left in order to see the old man better.

"Tahoe is it?" she asked. "I've already met the rest of the team, except you, wise seer." She paused, admiring something about him, something mystical and overwhelming. "I'm Susan Logan— the *other* Susan Logan."

Tahoe stepped forward, close enough to see her better. "It is quite troubling to make your acquaintance, but nonetheless astounding. I have seen many things in my years. You are a first of your kind. I have also seen you in my visions."

"I'm flattered," she said. "Good, I hope?"

"I'm afraid not." Tahoe politely bowed and stepped backward.

"Everyone, please be seated." Susan ushered the three of them to sit opposite Sidney and Leah, but to leave her room at the end of the couch, so she could still see her double face to face.

"Yes, gentleman, please be seated." The doppelganger echoed Susan. "But first, take a look inside the box on the coffee table." Brett, Dylan, and Tahoe stood and glanced inside the metal box. "That's your proof, gentlemen, of how far past the edge our dear Dr. Logan has slipped. That's *her* gun, not mine."

Tahoe glanced over at her.

"Luckily for you we made it here in time," he said.

She smirked at the old man as the three of them sat down. Susan stared at her blankly, waiting for her to begin.

"Well," Susan prompted. "We're all here. That's what you wanted. Now, let's hear it."

"I'm sorry, wait a minute," Sidney interrupted. He held his phone up, and then propped it up on the end table next to him, so that it would record her sitting in the adjacent chair. "I'm recording this. I don't care. She's not going to intimidate me. Besides, we can delete the videos if we need to."

"Agreed," Dylan said, holding his phone back up as well. Brett followed their actions, propping his phone up on the coffee table, where his camera captured her in a full frontal focus. "Susan, as chief-investigator, I'm ruling that it's not only imperative, but essential to your safety that we have some type of video documentation of this moment. It would be unwise not to."

Susan lifted her hands up in frustration and defeat.

"Suit yourselves, boys," the doppelganger said. "I truthfully don't want to begin this meeting with animosity. I'd like to speak, hopefully, to make you all understand, but in order for you to understand me better, I need you all to realize *who* I am, and what this world has come to mean to me. My intention was never to hurt Susan or anyone else. What happened to Taryn Page was not my doing. That was Angus' work."

She turned her focus to Susan, who continued staring at her intently.

"All I knew when I came into being was that I was *you*," she said. "All I understood was that we were the same person, somehow split in dual worlds. Angus led me to believe that you were my other half, and in order for me to be complete, to be free of the blue realm was for you to walk through the Black Mirror and join us. I didn't understand your reluctance, your fear when you entered. When you collapsed, I assumed you were no more." She glanced in Brett's direction. "As Mr. Taylor so aptly put it, I was a 'newborn.'

"When Angus brought me through the Black Mirror, and I entered into this world, I assumed *this* was my life now. It was a brilliant, vibrant, and beautiful world that I had suddenly been reborn into. How could I have ever wanted to go back?"

"But certainly Angus explained to you that I was your host and that you lived as long as I lived," Susan interjected. "At that point you *knew* we were two separate beings."

A slight twinge of guilt and embarrassment sunk her lower lip into a frown.

"And if you had gone back through the Black Mirror and into the blue realm, you would have ceased to exist, as my own doppelganger had." Leah's conclusion was correct, as far she knew.

"I could never have gone back," she said. "Eventually, Susan's fear of the blue realm had become my own. Imagine yourself being me, born into this world for the first time, not of a natural birth, but as an adult human injected into a marvelous world full of color, people, and fresh air abounding. As I matured, the more and more I became Susan."

"Because Susan's thoughts became your own," Brett pointed out.

"Precisely," she said, her tone turning slightly sharper. How strange they failed to see where this was all heading. As if their own sins and transgressions washed over them like holy water. "Once Susan was free of the blue realm, for me, returning would not have been possible. The gateway was destroyed, remember? So, why couldn't Susan and I coexist?"

"Because you lived your life as *me*," Susan said. "There could not have been two of us! You lived off of me, used my identity, not to mention embezzled my money."

"But that's just it, Susan. She doesn't understand." Now, Brett spoke up once again. "As a newborn into this world, she had no conception of money, or value. How could she? She doesn't fully realize what she's done."

"Well, I sure as hell did," Susan said, turning her head towards him.

"So you stopped me by claiming your identity had been stolen, and you were right," she said. "But I did get to see much of this world in its beautiful splendor. I've been to New York and witnessed its bustling, thriving magnificence."

"Yes, I know," Susan replied curtly.

"So, when the trail we picked up on went cold, it was because you knew we were on to you. Am I right?" Dylan asked.

She nodded. "When I used a credit card Susan reported stolen, I was almost arrested. Luckily for me, I faded into my ghostly form for quite a while, disappearing without a trace. Another reason for the dead end, Mr. Rasche, is because Susan's thoughts began to give her away." She paused and glanced at each one of them. "In more ways than you can imagine."

Sidney loomed in closer toward her. "Which I assume, brings us to the point of this meeting?"

"You assume, correctly, Mr. Pratt," she said, and then turned her gaze to each of them. "Or may I call you all by your first names? After all, we already know each other well enough."

"Go right ahead," Leah said.

The doppelganger crossed her hands in front of her, a habit that belonged to Susan.

"The more I matured, the more Susan and I merged together. Everything about her became imprinted upon me, and not just her thoughts but her memories, feelings, emotions, cognitions, and even her past studies. Aspects and definitions suddenly appeared in my mind to words like 'parapsychology' and 'psychosomatic.' But memories are memories. They weren't just imprinted, they were ingrained. Memories of Tracy Kimball, of Roman Hadley; aka, her beloved Mark, and of course, that awful night in Cedar Manor and the cover-up that followed."

She watched their faces turn toward one another. She noticed the glint of fear in their shifting eyes which grew suddenly wider.

"And then there was that one night. You know what night I'm

referring to, Skinwalker." Gasps expelled around her. She sat staunchly, achieving her desired effect. Brett simply stared at her, shocked by her turning on him. Susan closed her eyes and shook her head. "What was it the demon called you that night in Cedar Manor, 'shifter?' I know all about that night, Brett. I even know the burial spot. You told Susan everything in your sessions.

"But Susan, I must say, that press conference you held to stave off the Men in Black was brilliant." She turned her gaze toward Dylan. "The rest of the world doesn't know the details of your abduction that night, do they, Dylan? Such an amazing story, you may have to share it with the world sooner than you think."

"Get to your point," Susan ordered.

"My point is this, Susan. How about if I tell the world about Taryn Page, and how I came to be? I know *everything*, Susan. I know about Dean Collier. And I also know Tom Goddard would love to hear what really happened to Dean's daughter, Lydia. But worse, if I tell them what happened to that poor soul buried beyond the Taylor farmhouse, you may all be looking at murder and accessory charges. Are you all following me?"

"You bitch," Susan hissed.

"Likewise, Dr. Logan."

"So what is your ultimatum?" Tahoe asked.

She sat back, now that the worst of it was over.

"What I want is simple. I want to remain free to live out my existence. You all will provide me with another name and identity, and also the means for which I'm supposed to live. In exchange, I agree to never contact Susan or any of you ever again. I will safely become another one of your little secrets. As far as the likeness goes, we'll call it a coincidence. Many people in this world look alike, or so I've gathered. What is it they say, 'Everyone has a twin?'"

"And if we don't agree?" Sidney asked.

"Then I fill Detective Goddard in on everything, especially the skinwalker."

Susan was about to speak, but Dylan interrupted her.

"*If* we agree to your terms, before that happens, I have a question for you, and so does Tahoe."

She sat forward and clapped her hands together in anticipation. "Ask away."

Dylan had set the EVP device on the table beside his phone. He pushed it forward in her direction. "This is a recording we captured a few nights ago in an abandoned cemetery. We'd like you to listen to it for just a moment."

"I'm all ears," she said.

Dylan pressed a button on the device and played the recording, then stopped and fast forwarded it. Once again, they listened to a ghostly voice call out Susan's name.

"*SU-SAN.*"

Dylan stopped the recording. "The voice we just heard, was it you?"

She shook her head. "No. My voice and Susan's are the same. Did that voice sound like either of us?"

Dylan glanced from one member of the team to another. She could tell from the expression on his face; he knew she was right. The ensuing silence assured her that no one disagreed.

"Tahoe, I believe you had a question," she said.

Tahoe told her about the murky, yellowish-brown haze surrounding her and Susan in his visions. "It is the color associated with unclean spirits, the restless, wandering dead."

"I'm not sure I have a soul, Tahoe," she said. "I am part of Susan, yet the soul belongs to her. Besides, do I look dead to you?"

Tahoe lowered his head. She spoke the truth, and this fact was an unwelcome one.

"And just how do you figure we could provide you with another identity?" Susan steered the conversation back to the obvious question.

"Since your skinwalker is a master of technology, I'm sure he'll have no trouble forging the appropriate forms of identification. As far as financial sustenance, between you and Dylan, you're both going to sort of 'buy me' out."

"Bullshit!" Sidney shouted. "She'll keep coming back. We'll never be rid of her."

"And if we don't," Leah exclaimed, "we could all be in big trouble."

The doppelganger held her hands up in a plea. "I assure you, I want this charade to be over as much as the rest of you. I have no ulterior motive. As I've explained, I just want to be free."

Susan rose from the couch. Anger burned her face a fiery red.

"I say you all let me handle this the way I originally planned." Susan's voice was a cold, harsh, monotone. "Doing away with her would not be the same as what happened at the farmhouse. There would be no body left to bury."

She felt Susan's anger and matched it. "How dare you?" She planted her hands firmly on the arms of the chair. "You're responsible for my existence! I wouldn't be here if you'd stayed away from that mirror! Your curiosity provoked me and summoned me into this world. It's you—you are the problem! You're responsible for every mishap, every tragedy, and every scandal that surrounds you and your team. You know it, I know it, and so do they!"

Suddenly, the people and objects surrounding her turned blurry, fuzzy. Faces faded into near obscurity. Something was happening to her. She felt a great weight bearing down upon her and an inner wrenching of something moving inside her, something attempting to tear her apart. She tried to slip into her ghostly form but failed. The overwhelming weight became a force, anchoring her down and preventing her from the task. She mustered all her strength and wriggled herself into a standing position, the ceiling lights glaring down upon her. She struggled to speak, yet her voice was lost.

"HE—HEL—"

"My God, what's happening to her?" Leah cried.

Her lips felt paralyzed, her senses taken prisoner. Susan's doppelganger stood speechlessly beckoning them. Finally, she managed a long, agonizing groan.

14

THE WRONG SUSAN

THE BULLET HAD RIPPED THROUGH LAUREN'S SKULL.
Blood and bits of brain splattered the walls. Her body slumped to
the floor with a resounding thud. Abruptly, the spirit was expelled
from Lauren's body with a force much akin to the pistol's
kickback. The sense of heat the spirit felt during the possession
became replaced by the chill of its own wandering soul.

Ghostly eyes absorbed the grizzly scene. Eugene and Lauren lay
sprawled, dead on the floor. It would be deemed a murder-suicide.
Now, silence pervaded the room in the form of final judgment. An
ominous truth seemed to blare through the quiet. Two lives had
been stolen, but what was done was done. Vengeance had been
accomplished, yet it was not over. It was just beginning.

The spirit felt no vindication. The need for vengeance
remained. The rage continued, but somewhere underneath, the
spirit sensed a silent cry, an unacknowledged plea for rest as if its
entire being remained trapped in a dual consciousness.
Beleaguered by the continuous stream of emotions, the spirit
languished in its confusion, and then suddenly thrived as its
attention turned back to its goal—vengeance. It would find the
perfect host, one that would sustain it long enough. Then, with

human eyes, the spirit would look once more upon the world from which it had been so tragically ripped away.

The spirit abandoned the overwhelming flood of emotions. It let itself become swept up in the thick, tainted fog that enveloped it. Thick and murky, the fog enwrapped the spirit and carried it through time and space. As the fog dissipated, the spirit once again recognized its surroundings. It returned to the copper-toned brick house it left not long ago. Lingering high above it, the spirit soon found itself behind its thick, brick walls. Its thoughts had led it back here, to Susan's house, for its unfinished agenda.

But Susan was not alone. The spirit happened upon a tense and escalating scene in the living room. The young man and the girl from the funeral parlor were seated on one side of the sectional couch. Three men sat on the other side, two younger, and one older. It was the older man at the end who caught the spirit's attention. Much like the young woman with the long blonde hair, the old man exhibited a strange shimmering in the middle of his forehead. He was a seer, like the girl, but older and more practiced. What the spirit saw next not only added to its confusion but enthralled and provoked its attention. Susan sat at the opposite end of the couch from the old seer, but directly adjacent to Susan, another Susan sat in a chair.

The spirit was suddenly barraged with images: Susan being inside the house one moment, and then walking through the door the next, Susan leaving the house for work and then reappearing shortly after. Two Susans sat directly across from each other. Bewildered, the spirit watched as voices rose. It listened to the sound of tempers flaring.

"I say you all let me handle this the way I originally planned."

One Susan rose from the couch and towered over the other in the chair. The spirit heard and even felt the anger in a wave of heat that emanated from the Susan who stood. The Susan who sat in the chair retorted.

"How dare you?" She slammed her hands down on the arms of the chair. *"You're responsible for my existence!"*

Existence, what did she mean by existence? The spirit heard words jumbled together, words it failed to conjoin and comprehend. The Susan in the chair blamed the other, something about a mirror, a mishap, and a tragedy. The spirit moved toward the Susan in the chair. Her words became irrelevant, dying away as the spirit noticed something about her. Something was different, yet the spirit had encountered her before.

Coldness as it neared her. It remembered now, the cold, hard shell of a human it had met in the living room. It sought to invade her, but their meeting had been interrupted. Now, that same coldness drew the spirit closer to her. She was so unlike any other human. No physical human warmth emanated from her. It had to possess her. It had to find out.

The spirit mustered its energy into a whirlwind of flight and bore down upon her, immersing itself in her. It felt itself merging with her coldness. In through her soft flesh, in through her drawing breath, the spirit invaded her. Her blood was cold, her body devoid of a heartbeat. Through a doppelganger's eyes, the spirit glanced out at frightened faces.

This woman was not Susan. How could she be? The spirit anchored itself inside her, but the strange host fought profoundly. She stabled herself into a standing position and attempted to cry out for help.

"My God, what's happening to her?" The blonde girl asked.

The doppelganger uttered a long frightening groan, but the spirit soon overwhelmed her. Now, it was in control. It gazed at the Susan standing in the middle of the room, the real Susan. She stood trembling, her hand clasping her collar. The spirit raised its host's arm and pointed at Susan with a long index finger.

"Susan!"

Cries and gasps sounded throughout the small circle. The spirit heard the guttural growl that escaped its host, the rough, coarse tone of the dead, yet the voice did not belong to its host. *It* surpassed her vocal chords and spoke freely, but time and death had erased its everyday ease of natural speech.

Susan's guests rose to their feet. The men were standing, aiming their phones at the possessed woman. The old seer was quick, pointing and calling out what he naturally saw.

"She is possessed, Susan," he cried. "Stand away from her. Within her is the malevolent spirit I have foreseen, the murky, foggy haze, the unclean soul."

The spirit turned its host's head ever so slightly. It looked upon the old seer as it adjusted to the strange woman's eyes. Its eyesight grew clearer and clearer. The murky, foggy haze the seer so aptly described dissipated the longer the spirit remained in the host. For a moment the spirit glimpsed the old seer, and then a younger Indian chief, and then the old seer again. The spirit saw new life within the old man, rejuvenation, time standing still.

"You would make the perfect host, old man," it croaked. "Time has stopped for you. But you are not part of my plan." It turned its attention back toward Susan, still pointing the doppelganger's finger. "Lydia's dead because of you!"

"Who the hell are you?" Susan yelled. "What in God's name have you to do with Lydia?"

The spirit attempted to answer her. It sought to speak a name Susan would clearly remember—Dean. It attempted to speak, a task that became easier with each passing word. Yet this time, something interrupted this action. Inhabiting its host's body, the spirit suddenly felt the strangest feeling of being torn apart, a rumbling inside, as if the host was rejecting its presence. Now, through its host's eyes, the spirit saw double, two of everything as the dual personage it created was being abruptly separated. What kind of being had it inhabited? The spirit had been allured by her, drawn to this aberration in its errant curiosity. It had chosen unwisely; it had chosen the wrong Susan.

The head of its host drew back and out of her mouth bellowed a long, agonizing groan. The spirit felt its grip loosening. The being it inhabited was a ghostly one, one that was slipping away from its grasp. Suddenly, the world turned blurry, fuzzy, and cold again. The spirit had been evicted by its host. Now, the wandering spirit watched its host drop to the floor. Then, she began to fade in and out of reality.

––––––––

SOMETHING HAD OVERCOME HER. SOME STRANGE FORCE suddenly invaded this human shell she so effortlessly adorned. She felt it inside her, trying to weigh her down. Rising unsteadily to her feet, she fought back. She tried to slip into her ghostly form and eject its presence, but the invader would not allow her. She called out, but the malevolence inside her subdued her ghostly essence into pitch blackness. Undoubtedly, the wayward being failed to understand; she was not human. It could not possess her as it could human beings. She was a copy, a counterfeit designed in an alternate realm this beautiful world could not see.

Yet the fight was hard. She struggled against the strange force's overwhelming presence. It saw with her eyes and heard with her ears. She witnessed images of Tahoe, visions of his dual soul. The old man was inhabited, much like she was in this moment, though it was not the same type of possession. She swam vigorously through a sea of darkness. She fought against the spirit's domination, but not without a price.

The doppelganger realized something as she and the spirit battled against each other. The ghostly form she fiercely sought to escape by was in essence, her soul. As their battle raged, the calamitous thrashing of souls caused her outer human shell to be ripped apart from the inside. The battle scars would leave irreparable damage.

She ejected the spirit from her, but it was too late. She fell to floor and felt her ghostly form escaping. It was over. Her time had come to an end. The beautiful world she'd grown so fond of grew darker and darker.

––––––––

BRETT COULD NOT BELIEVE HIS EYES, EVEN THOUGH he'd seen it happen before. Susan's doppelganger lay writhing on the floor, fading in and out as he and the others stood in shock, recording the incident with their phones. The woman who had just blackmailed them met an unexpected fate, accosted by something they failed to see, something that mistook her for Susan.

Tahoe was right; she was possessed. The angry malevolence inside her had lashed out at Susan and even mentioned Lydia. Somehow it had to be a clue to this thing or spirit's identity. Whatever it was that took possession of the doppelganger was about to name itself, but the doppelganger had fought it rigorously, only to be destroyed in the end. Sounds of astonishment surrounded him. Susan's doppelganger gradually faded, dissipating into a mere silhouette that lingered for a moment, and then vanished.

Voices overlapped behind him; all except Susan's. From the corner of his eye, Brett saw her holding her hand over her mouth and simply staring at the spot where her doppelganger had fallen. Brett felt the day's tension mounting inside him. He said nothing. The doppelganger's attempt to extort them, dangling him as a weapon, and then her sudden and subsequent demise unexpectedly triggered something inside him.

He felt the chaos, the desire to shift, the need to disassociate from the situation and run free through the hills. Yet there were no hills here in King's Haven. The sweat blanketed his forehead and trickled down his temples. The change was commencing, and he stood powerless against it.

———

SHE WAS GONE—FOREVER.

Susan witnessed her doppelganger bravely battle an unseen presence, and then collapse to the floor. Surprised by a mixture of shock, relief, and pity, Susan watched her disappear like a ghost.

The third known doppelganger to escape from the depths of the Black Mirror had vanished in front of them. This time, they had several different camera-phone recordings of the same event. Each one would be catalogued within the society's archives.

Susan lingered in silent shock as it all transpired. Then, just before her doppelganger fell to floor, Susan felt a great tugging inside, like something had been torn away from inside her. Perhaps the other Susan was right. Perhaps they shared the same soul.

Susan remained convinced that whatever had taken possession of her doppelganger had come for *her*. She'd seen it in the doppelganger's eyes, how differently they appeared within seconds, and how those piercing, glaring eyes searched around the room for her. Under the malevolent spirit's possession, the doppelganger pointed adamantly at her and called out her name. Then, it blamed her for Lydia's death.

A notion of someone familiar suddenly swept Susan, but no, she told herself it was impossible. A chill tickled her spine. One thing remained certain; the malevolent spirit had destroyed her doppelganger. Susan continued to stare at the spot where she'd fallen, knowing well that her demise was not meant as a favor, but as a warning.

"Holy shit!" Sidney cried.

"The last of the doppelgangers, gone," Dylan observed. Then, he walked over to Susan and wrapped his arm around her shoulder. "Are you okay?" Susan nodded. "Listen everyone, I believed her when she said the voice we recorded on the EVP was not her. I wasn't convinced the voice belonged to her from the start, but I had to eliminate her as a possibility. Obviously, Tahoe's right. We're dealing with something far more sinister, a malevolent of some type."

"I know what we all saw." Leah, like the rest had risen from the couch. Her eyes moved in all directions, searching for the unseen. "But my third eye isn't seeing anything in this room."

"That's because the spirit has removed itself for the moment," Tahoe said. "No doubt it will return."

"Then we need to get Susan out of here," Sidney argued.

Brett interrupted the murmurs of agreement. "Susan, it's happening," he said. "I feel it coming over me."

Susan took one look at him and saw the sweat glazing his face, the glossy look in his eyes, and the sudden luminous appearance of his skin. Brett was shifting. She had to help him.

"The backyard, Brett," she said. "No one will see you there."

Brett ran past her, into the kitchen, and out through the sliding glass doors to her backyard. Susan followed behind. She'd been helping him understand the skinwalker curse. Now, her own dilemma had induced the chaotic tension in Brett. He needed her right now, regardless of what was happening. Susan slid the glass doors shut behind Brett but continued to grip the door's handle. She stood gazing into her backyard, quietly disturbed by the notion that tonight would be filled with utter mayhem.

15

TWO SEPARATE BEINGS, ONE SOUL

UPON REACHING THE FRESH, OUTSIDE AIR, BRETT realized how quickly dusk had come upon them. The invigorating coolness of the night air swept him. Susan's vast backyard was not his natural sanctuary, yet it was private and isolated. Tall thick pines and bushy spruces fenced and shaded the well-groomed lawn. Brett fled to a small space hindered by a thicket of spruce trees as the inevitable change began.

He yanked off his shirt, pulled down his jeans, and stood naked as the cool air rippled his changing flesh. Shuddering, he dropped to his knees and doubled over until the palms of his hands flattened the moist grass. His body elongated and writhed into a squirming, wriggling shape. Within seconds, coarse hair shot from pores while wedge-shape ears sprouted from his morphing head. Brett's face protruded into the wolf's snout. Sharp, canine fangs jutted downward like small daggers. Then, the wolf hurled its head back and uttered a low, eerie moan.

Lowering its head and cowering, the wolf understood that it needed to exhibit restraint. This was not its native territory. Its safety depended upon confining itself to this grassy expanse while the others, safely inside, watched over it. It sensed no other humans, except those who stood watching through the glass doors.

The wolf lifted its head up to the darkening sky, examining the infinite stars that mapped millions of pathways across a never-ending blueprint. How rare it was to catch a fluffy white cloud still visible at nightfall, yet there it lingered, leagues above. Then, the wolf saw something else, something that wasn't supposed to be there.

A murky, discolored fog seemed to drift of its own accord. The wolf watched it rise from the chimney and linger high above the house. As it wafted, the fog masked the fluffy white cloud, making it appear a sickly yellowish-brown for a passing moment. The fog descended in the wolf's direction, looming closer and closer. The wolf let out a cry, one meant as a warning to those who heard it. The fog approached, seemingly taunting the wolf and provoking its canine instincts.

The wolf leaped up and down and spun in circles, crying out and attempting to avoid the yellowish haze now lingering above its head. The foggy haze seeped downward, surrounding the wolf with its murky, tainted thickness. The wolf became caught up in it, immersed in its density and blinded by its haziness. The wolf scuttled backward and forward, attempting to escape it, but the fog prevailed, almost as if it acted out of a conscious intention.

Somewhere deep inside the wolf, the soul of Brett Taylor recognized this moment for what it was, a vision that had come to pass. Yet the wolf continued to fight. Its cries turned to growls, as anger erupted from inside it. Then, the wolf felt the fog enter its body, seeping and invading it, threatening to evict its soul. Instantly, the wolf became part of the sickly colored fog, which anchored itself well within the wolf.

Enraged, the wolf uttered a deafening howl. The piercing hollow sound was a sudden eruption, the cry of a trapped and tortured soul. Deep inside, Brett Taylor's soul battled a faceless being, a wandering malevolent presence. The silent, sudden invader acted fast, overpowering its host and turning its inner rage outward. Then, the wolf charged toward the sliding glass doors with full galloping speed. Pouncing upward in a full frontal stance, the possessed wolf planted its paws on the glass doors and gazed at the faces behind it. Saliva seeping and dripping from its fangs, the wolf growled ferociously.

It recognized the woman behind the glass—Susan. Somehow, the wolf felt a simultaneous love and hatred toward her, yet the soul of Brett Taylor stirred upon seeing the old man who stood alongside her. The old man held out his hands, and the wolf heard him speak through the glass, heard him challenge the soul that fought inside. The sound of his voice shook the besieged soul into full awakening.

"Fight it, skinwalker! The malevolent presence has taken you prisoner. Fight it!"

Tahoe's voice thundered, enough to scatter demons.

———

THE SPIRIT'S CONFUSION THICKENED WHEN THE hapless shell of a human, lying broken and defeated, disappeared like a ghost. Then, inexplicably, the spirit found itself hovering high above the house once again. Below, a creature stalked the grounds, one that spotted its presence high above.

The spirit descended until it lingered just above the creature's head. It recognized the creature that roamed the vast lawn below, a wolf, but there was something extraordinary about this wolf. Uncommonly large, the wolf appeared docile until it recognized the hovering spirit for what it was. Growling, its head thrusting upward into the night air, here was yet another uncanny being, one that provoked the spirit's confusion, curiosity, and its malevolent intentions.

As it neared the wolf, the spirit sensed something much like it had when encountering the strange woman. The wolf was not a cold shell; the wolf had a soul. And equally unlike the woman, the spirit experienced the same sensations around the wolf as it did human beings. Something about the woman had not been human. Something about the wolf *was* human.

Enrapt, the spirit entered the raging wolf. It absorbed the wolf and anchored its own fury deep inside, manipulating the wolf's movements, thoughts, and actions. Suddenly, the spirit saw a face, dark hair, dark eyes, and a trimmed mustache and goatee. The face belonged to one of the young men in Susan's house. It was *his* soul that fought so fiercely, so valiantly against the invading spirit. *His* soul and the wolf's soul were one. The wolf and the young man were the same. Two separate beings, one soul. Just like the strange woman who shared Susan's soul.

The spirit gazed with the wolf's eyes toward the glass doors. Through the wolf, it would make its presence known yet again. Through the wolf, it would send another message. Mustering all of its rage and fury, the spirit charged the wolf's body forward with great canine speed, controlling the wolf with full and total possession.

Its message was for Susan. She stepped away from the doors as the wolf planted its paws on the glass, the old seer standing firmly alongside her. Then, the old man's voice boomed like thunder, and the spirit found itself floating once again, hovering above the changing form of a human man.

———

TAHOE STOOD BEHIND THE GLASS DOORS, HIS HANDS held out in front of him. The wolf dropped at the sound of his voice. Tahoe and Susan witnessed the skinwalker's change back to human form. After its hair and snout receded, the wolf morphed into a long larvae shape that writhed and wriggled into the blank, faceless form of a human. Within seconds, Brett lay face down on the back patio, naked and unresponsive.

"Sidney! Dylan! He needs your help," Tahoe called out.

Sidney, Dylan, and Leah gathered behind him and Susan at the glass doors. All of them bustling about to obtain a clear view of what was happening outside. As Tahoe yanked the sliding glass door open, Sidney ran outside and gathered up Brett's clothing, while Dylan turned Brett over, gently slapping the sides of his face to rouse him. Brett's eyes fluttered open, and they helped him into a standing position so he could dress. Then, they helped him inside.

"I'm alright, really," he said, a dazed faraway look in his eyes. "What exactly happened?"

"I called you out of the shifting, my friend," Tahoe said. "The wolf became possessed by the malevolent spirit that now seems to be warning us."

"Sit down," Susan advised. "I want to take your blood pressure."

"Really, Susan—" Brett began to protest.

"Sit!" she ordered. Retrieving her black bag from a hallway closet, Susan listened to his heartbeat with her stethoscope. Then, she wrapped his upper arm and pumped the blood pressure machine, gazing at her watch as she did so. "Interesting, your heartbeat and blood pressure are slightly low but normal. This may be the cause of your euphoria after shifting."

"I remember something." Brett ignored her. "I remember seeing you through the glass and feeling something, something like hatred." Susan stared at him. "Whatever that thing is, it feels hatred toward you, a vengeful fixation. I felt it, although I don't recall much else."

"My guess is that this spirit is unable to possess that which is not human," Tahoe said. "The doppelganger was not human. She forced the spirit out when she tried to initiate her ghostly form. Yet the spirit was powerful enough to destroy her in the process."

"Maybe," Brett said. "But I'm human."

"*You* are human," Tahoe countered. "The wolf is not. In the case of the doppelganger, Susan was in possession of the soul, yet the spirit chose the wrong Susan. In your case, the spirit tried to possess a multifaceted soul, one that is shared with the wolf and other creatures. In essence, the wolf's soul was uncontrollable.

Like the doppelganger, the wolf rejected the wayward spirit's invasion."

Closing her black bag, Susan glanced up at them. "So, what exactly does all this mean? I'm assuming this malevolent being is going to continue to come after me?"

Tahoe hesitated, searching for the right words, until Brett intervened.

"Yes, it will. It was trying to send a message through the wolf. When the wolf charged toward the glass doors, it was trying to get to you. That I know."

"I'm afraid I agree," Tahoe said solemnly.

"Then that's it. It's settled." Sidney sounded adamant. He held up his hands, not wanting to hear more, as if the matter was already decided. "Susan has to leave here. She'll stay with one or more of us, so we can keep watch on her."

"She'll stay with me," Leah decided.

"Like hell!" Susan retorted. "What do you all think I'm going to do, run from this invisible presence for the rest of my life? What makes you all so convinced it won't follow me or even try to possess one of you? Don't forget, I'm also a paranormal investigator, with a degree in parapsychology. This thing is after *me*. So, I'm sure as hell going to find out what or who it is. I'll be damned if I'm going to be chased away from my home by some ghost, demon, poltergeist, or whatever the hell it is we're dealing with. I'm going to solve this dilemma once and for all. You all are either with me, or you're not."

"You're right, Susan," Dylan interjected. "Then that settles it. We're all staying here with you. We're going to discover what this presence is, together, like always."

Silence. Again, Tahoe searched carefully for the right words. Now was not the time to discuss the sensation he felt the moment he'd called out the possessed skinwalker. The feeling of lightning that surged through his body at that moment, how he'd closed his eyes and saw the face of his great-grandfather, the chief, striding towards him, the tingle of rejuvenation inside him. The details of how recent events somehow sparked this sudden change he felt would have to wait until later. Tahoe spoke, knowing one thing for certain.

"Then we will defeat this malevolence at all costs, and by doing so, all things will be revealed."

16

MY NAME IS DEAN

"SID, HOW MANY INFRARED CAMERAS DO WE HAVE?"
Dylan asked when he, Brett, and Sidney stood huddled, assessing
the situation.

"I have only one in the van," Sidney replied.

"We're going to need more."

After retrieving the single infrared video camera from the van,
Brett set it up in Susan's living room. Then, Sidney drove him back
to the farmhouse to obtain two more cameras. That was two hours
ago. In that time, Brett grabbed a change of clothes for himself and
for Tahoe, but not before slipping into the shower and washing the
skinwalker sweat and slime from his body. Sidney then drove to
his place for a quick shower and an overnight bag. Now, they
returned Susan's, ready to set up the cameras for a ghostly night
watch.

"As I'm sure you all know, infrared video cams allow us to pick
up ghostly presences on film, often in the shape of a mist, a fog,
even a face, or a shape of some kind." Brett instructed while
setting up the second camera in Susan's kitchen. A flash of
memory swept his mind, the wolf's memory, the presence of a

yellowish-fog or haze lingering above. "These three cameras will serve as monitors, as well as recorders."

"I've set up the EVP monitor, as well, to pick up sounds," Dylan said.

Brett turned to Susan, realizing she'd seen the full effect of his shifting earlier. At least now, she'd have a visual image when she read the journal he'd been keeping at her request.

"I'm sorry, Susan, but the third camera has to go in your bedroom. Sleep is a crucial time for any presence that seeks to invade."

"He's right," Tahoe spoke up. "It is also not wise for you to sleep in your room alone. It would defeat the purpose of our being here."

"I'll stay with her," Leah opted.

"But you need to sleep also," Sidney said. "I say we sleep in shifts watching over her. Leah, you and I can decide between first and second shifts."

Susan sighed. "Is that really necessary? I doubt I'll get much sleep tonight anyway."

"It is," Dylan replied. "You decided to find out what this thing is, so that's what we're doing. I want to go as far as even luring this thing out."

"I'm afraid there will be no need." Tahoe's tone took on a dire graveness, one he often used when foreshadowing trouble. "It will return. I'm sure of it."

———

SUSAN, DYLAN, AND BRETT OVERSAW THE SETUP OF THE bedroom camera, and then the entire team adjourned to the living room. The night wore on, yet they sat tirelessly conversing, wondering, and waiting for something unseen.

"You know, I'm still overwhelmed by the fact that she's gone," Susan began. "I'm finally rid of her. But her quick and sudden demise was meant to be mine. Now I'm left to deal with a faceless, bodiless entity, if that's even the right word because we don't know exactly what we're dealing with yet. But we all agree on one thing, and that is the malevolent nature of this being."

"It is, in fact, a spirit," Tahoe decreed, "a spirit tainted by some form of malevolence."

"What's stumps me," Sidney said, "is that many experts claim that malevolent spirits are unable to possess humans."

"Nonsense," Tahoe rebutted. "Malevolent spirits may not be able to anchor themselves inside the host as long as demons can, but they may possess the host just as forcefully and as powerfully."

Susan sat wondering if now was the time to mention the odd premonition she felt earlier. They all sat staring at her, knowing as well as she did that this thing had some connection to her. It called out her name in the cemetery. Its presence was witnessed here in her house.

"Susan, are you sure you can't think of any reason why this thing is attached to you?"

Dylan was onto her. There was no need to continue dismissing her earlier notion.

"Throughout all of this, I kept thinking of Dean." Susan looked at each of them as she spoke, attempting to decipher their reactions. "Let's keep in mind that to us, nothing is impossible. This spirit mentioned Lydia's name. You all heard it blame me for her death. I also keep thinking of the word Lydia used when describing Dean's radical change in behavior—malevolent."

"A tainted soul stained of the sickly color of sin, the sin of suicide," Tahoe reflected. "That is entirely possible."

"Then this eerie notion becomes more plausible by the moment," Susan said. "I still wonder what Lauren was referring to when she mentioned this childhood incident of Dean's. I wonder what happened to him. What was it that was so horrible he failed to mention it in his adulthood? Of all the opportunities to discuss and explore this questionable event, why had he not taken advantage of it and told me?"

Susan stroked her chin with her index finger, turning an idea over in her mind.

"I think it's inevitable," she said. "First thing tomorrow, I need to find out how to contact Lauren. We need to find out what that childhood incident was, and why it was hidden throughout Dean's life. It may hold the key to this mystery. I think she can be trusted. We should consider letting in her in on what's going on."

"That will be tricky," Leah said. "How do we discuss this without mentioning the shadows and their role in all this?"

"We don't," Susan replied. "I'll simply explain that I was Dean's psychiatrist, and that it concerns me. I will mention that I suspect I'm being haunted, and that Dean is somehow connected. She did approach us and ask if we were paranormal investigators. Perhaps this time the truth may be the best approach."

She watched them glance at one another, nodding and shrugging.

"It can't hurt," Brett said. "You're right. We don't have to mention the shadows. All she needs to know is what's happening right now."

"Yeah," Sidney agreed. "Worst case scenario—she thinks we're a bunch of loons."

"I'll start by calling the funeral parlor tomorrow," Susan said. "If they won't give me her number, I'll leave mine for her to contact me. I have to talk to her. Lauren holds the key to all this in more ways than we know."

"What if this malevolent spirit is *not* that of Dean Collier?" Dylan asked.

Susan cast her eyes down in defeat, and then glanced back up at him.

"Then God help us all."

———

THE SPIRIT FOLLOWED THE SOUND OF THEIR VOICES. IT heard the mentioning of its name. It seeped slowly downward, resting and lingering just above their heads. It watched them as it listened. Susan. The three men, one of whom could change his human form, one whose face it had seen inside the wolf host. The girl and the old man sat placidly, shimmering eyes in the middle of their foreheads. Again, it heard the spoken sound of its earthly name—*Dean*.

Then, the old seer spoke. *"A tainted soul stained of the sickly color of sin, the sin of suicide."*

Suicide. Fire, blood, the taste of gunpowder, and then blackness.

"I still wonder what Lauren was referring to when she mentioned this childhood incident of Dean's. I wonder what happened to him."

Susan's words stirred the spirit away from the memory.

"What was it that was so horrible—?"

Her voice trailed off into an echo. *"Horrible, horrible, horrible..."*

The spirit saw a stream of memories: the boy it had once been, strapped down to the bed, bloodshot eyes, a menacing glare, convulsions, screaming, a priest making the sign of the cross. The memory was real, just as real as the suicide memory. Silently, the spirit raged. The past, a pain it had fought hard to forget. Susan made it come alive again not only with her words, but her interference. It would make her pay. It would make them all pay.

The spirit sought the center of its ghostly energy and mustered its strength, a task it had now mastered. It surged toward its target, Susan, who sat on the couch idly talking.

"I have to talk to her. Lauren holds the key to all this in more ways than we know."

But Lauren was dead, and Susan was next. There would be no talking.

Their voices continued.

"What if this malevolent spirit is not that of Dean Collier?"

This time, the spirit's full earthly name was mentioned, a possible malevolent spirit. So they knew. But the dead will tell no tales, and the living will have no proof.

"Then God help us all."

The spirit lunged at Susan, bringing a sudden breeze in its wake. It neared her, close enough to touch her, to invade her. Then, the young man with the gypsy look and the shifting soul bounded up from the opposite end of the couch.

"We've got something on video! It's here in this room!"

The spirit whisked itself away amid the ensuing confusion. Up toward the high cathedral ceiling it soared, issuing a gale force wind so strong it spun the ceiling fan and swayed the chandelier in the dining room. Its rampage was interrupted, for now.

———

FOLLOWING BRETT'S LEAD, THE ENTIRE TEAM POUNCED up from their sitting positions, planting their feet on the floor, their eyes searching around them. An invisible invader roamed silently among them.

"I saw it on the monitor," Brett exclaimed. "A haze seeped into the camera's view."

"I saw it too," Dylan said. "It's gone now, but the camera should've recorded it."

"Notice the ceiling fan." Leah pointed above her head. The ceiling fan, set on the off position, spun swiftly on its own. "And the dining-room chandelier is swaying. The spirit created that gust of wind we felt. It's powerful enough to cause physical disturbances."

"Which means it's reached the poltergeist level," Sidney concluded.

Tahoe searched the ceiling with his eyes, hoping to catch sight of the elusive haze.

"All right, everyone, let's sit back down," Susan suggested. "The last thing we should do is let it intimidate us."

Brett sat and flipped open his laptop, revealing a triple screen view captured by the three infrared cameras. The others clustered around him. He clicked on the box displaying the living-room view, enlarged the image, and then rewound the video. They caught a strange misty haze rolling backwards. Then, Brett clicked playback.

On the video, Susan asked God to help them all. That's when the haze seeped towards her. Brett had alerted everyone, and then the misty haze swooshed away from Susan and rolled up toward the high ceiling. Now, everyone turned their eyes away from the video and up toward the ceiling as Tahoe had, knowing that the invisible invader lurked somewhere within.

"It's here," Susan said, her eyes still roving the ceiling. "I can feel it. It's me it wants. You all saw the video. Now, we must wait."

"There must be something we can do to make this thing move on," Leah observed. "This is frustrating. I'm seeing nothing."

"That's because it's elusive, Little One," Tahoe said. "It knows what you and I are."

"I say we smoke this thing out, draw it out into the open and expose it." Sidney went on to suggest that bringing the spirit out and confronting it could weaken its hold over the situation.

"Yes, confrontation is inevitable," Tahoe countered. "And then what? I doubt any of us holds the power of exorcism over this thing. The shadows were a different story. We were able to see them. They influenced and manipulated. This spirit exudes the power of both life and death, a life which it has not yet given up, and a death it has not yet accepted."

"DEAN!" Susan bellowed his name as loud as she could. Her voice carried through the house, bouncing off the walls and creating a soft echo that traveled upward. "So you blame me for Lydia's death?" She continued to shout up toward the ceiling, her eyes searching above her methodically. "Don't blame me, Dean. Blame the shadows! I didn't kill her! But if it's me you want, then *come and get me!"*

The six of them stood waiting, listening to the silent maddening sound of nothing.

———

OUTSIDE, THE GREAT STARRY EXPANSE DARKENED TO A deep indigo. The moon grew brighter, illuminating a deep blue ring around its core. The celestial sight was proof to the spirit that time had shifted forward into twilight. Yet inside, those who gathered remained restless, sleepless, keeping vigilant watch throughout the night.

The spirit hovered atop the staircase, watching them, listening to their words. With a bird's eye view it witnessed their diligence, their lack of fear, their determination to fight.

"Sidney and Leah will guard your room in shifts." The young man with the curly black hair addressed Susan. "Tahoe will take the room next to yours. Brett and I will sleep in shifts in the room down the hall. Whoever is awake will keep watch down here and maintain the cameras."

"I have some extra pillows and blankets upstairs," Susan insisted. "You all don't have to completely rough it, Dylan. Besides, I have to go up and get the rooms ready."

"I'll go with you," Leah offered.

Susan and Leah walked toward the staircase. The spirit watched them, recalling Susan's words as she shouted through the house, *"Come and get me."* Blame the shadows, she'd said. The shadows, at first she hadn't believed. Now, death trailed in their wake.

The two women ascended from the foot of the staircase, step by step, higher and higher. The spirit sensed a wave of human heat as they neared. Closer and closer they approached. Susan would reach the top within seconds. Now was the time to destroy her life as she destroyed Lydia's. Now was the time to invade her, to claim her soul.

Susan arrived at the top, inhaling a deep breath and sighing. Moving like a powerful wind, the sprit entered her, seeping in through her heaving breath. It glimpsed her beating heart. It felt warmth from the heat inside her. Gazing through her eyes, it focused upon the soft light of the upstairs chandelier. The spirit manipulated Susan's legs slightly forward, careful to not lose balance at the top of the staircase. Susan's body wobbled slightly, her head lolling to the side. Finally, her body stood straight. The spirit had gained control. It anchored itself inside her.

The spirit stood inside its host, distracted by the voice that spoke from behind.

———

"SUSAN? ARE YOU OKAY?" SUSAN TOOK A DEEP BREATH and swayed after reaching the top of the staircase. Leah thought she was about to faint. Not a surprise, after the long day's events. "Susan?" Leah laid her hand on Susan's shoulder. Keeping her back turned, Susan flinched and pulled away. "Susan, what's wrong?" Leah asked.

Slowly, Susan turned around and faced her. Leah felt the strongest sense of déjà vu. Susan's face had taken on a sudden and unexplainable distortion. Her bloodshot eyes appeared the same as in the vision the shadows had shown Leah. Susan was possessed. The malevolent spirit was inside her.

"Guys!" Leah called out. "Dylan! Sidney!"

Susan's body hobbled forward. Leah tried to grasp the banister behind her but missed. A cold, hard hand belonging to Susan reached out and pushed her. Losing her balance, Leah tumbled down the stairs, head over heels, her arms flailing in failed attempts to break her fall. Plummeting, she screamed. That's when she felt Dylan's hands grasping her, stopping her rapid descent to the bottom.

"I got you," he said. "Are you okay?"

She felt slightly dizzy from the tumble, but otherwise all right. Another vision had come to pass. Thankfully the stairs were carpeted. Leah rubbed her head and pointed to the figure at the top of the stairs.

"It's inside her!" she yelled. "It overcame her at the top." Dylan pulled Leah up from the stairs and huddled her amid him and the others. All of them stood staring upward from the foot of the staircase. "That thing inside her pushed me, just like in the vision."

Slowly, Susan descended the stairs, bloodshot eyes projecting a menacing glare.

"Stop!" Sidney shouted. "Stay right where you are!"

"What have you done to Susan?" Brett asked.

Susan's face contorted into a grimace. Then, strange maniacal laughter grew louder and louder as it escaped her, yet it wasn't Susan's laughter, or even a woman's laughter. It was a man's laughter, the unbounded mirth of an insane man. The spirit inside was pleased with itself. It had found its way in.

Tahoe stepped in front of the younger men and addressed the spirit inside Susan.

"Malevolent spirit, who are you?"

The laughter abruptly stopped. Eyes that no longer resembled Susan's eyes glowered and focused on them from above, a distance of eight or nine steps.

"Haven't you already guessed who I am?" Rough like gravel, the spirit's voice rasped with a coarse and ragged intonation. Then, it shouted. "My name is Dean!"

17

POSSESSED

"SUSAN WAS RIGHT. YOU'VE COME BACK FOR vengeance."

Tahoe spoke to the spirit, grasping the banister with one hand and climbing three steps, a task he managed far more quickly and effortlessly than he would have only days earlier. He noticed Susan's face, instantly transformed, forlorn and haggard like in his visions. Her complexion waned to a sickly pale. Inside, the spirit was already taking a rapid toll on her.

"Yes." The spirit answered curtly. "You find me puzzling? I find you puzzling as well, old man. I see inside you. I see how your body rejuvenates, like a phoenix!"

Silently, Tahoe stood startled by the spirit's words, especially one in particular—phoenix. The spirit could see inside him, but Tahoe was not about to let the spirit gain the upper hand.

"If your vision is so acute, spirit, then why did you not see inside the doppelganger? You failed in your earlier possession. You latched onto a host you could not hold. Beware that you haven't repeated your mistake."

Again, the deranged hee-haw laughter echoed from the top of

the stairs. Susan's face squirmed and twisted. Her body folded into a sitting position on a top stair.

"I haven't," it said. "I'll release her when every fiber of her body has turned to rot!"

"Dean." Sidney stepped forward and stood over Tahoe's shoulder. The spirit just stared at him, not reacting to the mentioning of its name. "It wasn't Susan who killed Lydia. It was the shadows. You know it was the shadows."

"Who brought the shadows to Lydia? Susan did. *You* did." A possessed Susan pointed at Sidney. "I should break your neck before I break hers."

Sidney ignored the threat. Tahoe could feel the malevolence rolling from Susan in waves.

"Dean, did you tell Susan about the shadows all those years ago?" Dylan, standing at Tahoe's opposite side, asked the question loudly.

Tahoe noticed from the corner of his eye that Brett was redirecting the living room camera toward the staircase. He also noticed the record button on the EVP device was lit red.

"She failed to listen!" the spirit roared. Tahoe shook inside, hearing the coarse call of a dead man's voice coming from Susan. Then, the spirit's laughter erupted again. "Now, she knows. *You all* know."

Tahoe felt Sidney tugging him from behind. "Tahoe, step out of the way." Still silently stunned by the spirit's observations, Tahoe complied and stepped down so that Sidney stood in front, facing the figure seated atop the stairs. "Alright, everyone," Sidney said. "I'm going to ask. We have to find out, so here goes. Dean, what incident was Lauren referring to? What happened to you in your childhood?"

Susan's eyes grew wide, only they weren't Susan's. The bright blue orbs belonging to Susan Logan had drastically changed; they now appeared a deep aqua in color. Bloodshot tears drenched the whites of her eyes. Quickly, the figure leaped from the top stair and lunged toward Sidney. Descending the stairs in a flash, she assailed the small group. Susan's hand reached out, snatched Sidney's glasses from his face, and flung them over the staircase.

"I don't know! You tell me, you freak!"

Dylan and Sidney caught Susan's flailing hands and pinned her down, the spirit inside seething inches from their faces.

"Tell us, Dean." Off to the side of the staircase, Brett cajoled the spirit with his tone. "We can help you, but you must leave Susan."

The spirit's voice roared again as it struggled against them.

"I don't—kn—*ARRGH!*" The spirit recoiled, whiplashing Susan's head backward. "I can't—I can't—" Then, the spirit's voice changed, as if more than one person spoke. "Ask—Father —Maguire!"

The spirit writhed and seethed, twisting Susan's body with convulsive movements and banging her head off the stairs. Using his other hand, Dylan grasped the back of Susan's head, blocking the blows.

"Did you hear that?" Leah asked. "It sounds like there's more than one inside her." She turned to Tahoe. "Are we dealing with demons?"

"Not demons, Little One," he replied. "The malevolent spirit has mentioned itself by name, something a demon will not do. But you're right. I sense a duality with this spirit."

The voice inside Susan shouted again, but this time, words overlapped. Some words were whispered, some spoken loudly, leaving the team with only intermittent clues to decipher.

"Find—kill—her—priest—help—Fools!—me—Elysium."

"What does all this mean? What are you trying to say?" Brett coaxed the spirit.

"There's no point in hiding the truth," Dylan warned. "We're going to find Lauren."

Again, laughter ensued, a repetitive, maniacal, and seemingly triumphant giggle. Then, abruptly, Susan's face formed a seething, viperous mask.

"No need." The spirit spit its words, spewing spite like venom. "Lauren's dead!"

Then, the voice stopped. Susan's body stopped fighting. Her eyes rolled back; her head lolled off to the side.

"My God, is she—?" The sound of panic rose in Sidney's voice.

"No, she's not dead," Dylan said.

Leah stepped in between them. She lifted Susan's wrist and felt for a pulse, and then touched Susan's forehead. She bent down and placed her ear to Susan's chest. "She's unconscious but breathing."

"Let's carry her up to her bedroom," Dylan proposed. "We're going to have to tie her down to the bed."

"Oh, no," Leah exclaimed.

"We must, Leah," Sidney said. "We have no other choice. As long as that thing is inside her, it will turn her violent. Your little trip down the stairs could've been much worse. This spirit could harm Susan physically, and there's no telling to what extent. We have to secure her, to keep her safe."

Dylan lifted Susan's right arm and wrapped it around his neck. Cradling his arm beneath her shoulders and his other arm under her knees, he carefully stood while lifting her up in his arms. The others stood closely behind him. One by one, they ascended the stairs to Susan's bedroom where Dylan gently laid her on the bed.

"I worry about her unconscious state," Tahoe said. "The longer she remains unaware, the more the spirit can absorb her." Tahoe paused. "The more it absorbs her, the greater the chance to destroy her body."

"Then the harder we have to work to drive that thing out of her." Leah sounded determined, but a slight quiver in her voice gave away the fear that lay hidden underneath.

"We have a camera set up in here," Brett said. "She'll be monitored at all times. Everything that takes place in this room will be picked up by the camera."

"So what are we going to use to restrain her?" Sidney looked around, noticing nothing that would prove useful.

Dylan unbuckled his belt from his waist, issuing Sidney an upward nod. "Sid, your belt." Sidney followed Dylan's prompt and unfastened his belt. "We're going to have to use these to restrain her, at least for now."

Dylan fastened his belt around Susan's right foot, which he then secured to the bedpost. Sidney did the same to Susan's opposite foot.

"The rest of us aren't wearing belts," Brett said. "Leah, look and see if Susan has any. I don't think we're going to find anything like rope or power cords in this house. It will take too long to search anyway. We can't waste time."

Leah whisked open Susan's closet doors and frantically searched. "Belts, belts, belts." She whispered to herself, while rummaging through Susan's clothes. Finally, she saw them hanging against one of the closet doors. "Here, these are thinner, but they should work just the same."

"They're going to have to suffice," Dylan said, taking them from her. He and Brett secured Susan's wrists to the headboard posts as best they could.

Tahoe watched the spectacle in front of him. Susan looked like a classic case of possession, strapped down to the bed for her own safety, a scene straight from a horror movie. More and more of her color drained, leaving her healthy tan complexion to fade like a withering flower. Susan remained helplessly unconscious as the malevolent spirit dwelled inside her. Tahoe stood over Susan's bound, defenseless body, wondering what hell her soul was enduring.

WITHOUT WARNING, SUSAN WAS PLUNGED INTO TOTAL darkness. Somewhere near the top of the stairs, she'd taken a deep breath, and then the world around her turned black. Had she died? It seemed like the most logical answer. Her body felt free, listless. Her feet never touched the ground as she moved. She seemed to fly, yet it felt normal, even natural. But the pitch blackness was unnerving. This was not the blue realm. No extinct birds flew above her. There were no hellish opposites, no icy chill amid an everlasting dawn, only an eclipsing darkness through which she freely and ceaselessly glided. Maybe this was the end of her life.

A trickling of light penetrated the blackness, slowly widening until it overwhelmed and swallowed the darkness. Was she dreaming? Like most dreams, the blackness changed into a scene. Abruptly, she found herself standing in her old office again. She remembered it well with its freshly painted walls, the thick carpeting of a soft, soothing blue, and the infamous couch shared by a variety of patients strategically situated just opposite her desk. This was her office at the Meadowbrook Institution.

A male patient lay on the couch, his eyes fixated upon the ceiling. Susan was not close enough to make him out perfectly, but her instincts served her well. She moved closer to the couch, keeping her eyes on the man as he slowly rose upward into a sitting position. Now, she stood only inches from the couch, watching intently as the man slowly turned his head toward her. There was no mistaking his brownish-red hair or those piercing green eyes. Dean Collier glanced at her with a pleading expression, one that certainly didn't appear malevolent. It was the same expression she'd seen on Dean's face before, troubled, helpless, frantic, and what she once mistakenly deemed as paranoid. His chest heaved up and down, a frequent reaction when his mind became fraught with anxiety.

"Susan," he pleaded. His voice climbed with a burgeoning fear. "The shadows—why didn't you listen?"

"I'm sorry, Dean." Susan was quick, telling him what she wanted to say since the day he died. "I'm so sorry I failed you." Her voice creaked. Tears welled in her eyes. "How I wish I could go back and do it all over again. How I wish I could've saved you."

"Susan, the shadows brought it all back to me."

"Brought *what* back to you, Dean?"

Something within the corner of her eyeshot distracted her. She turned her head quickly and saw a young boy standing in the corner of the room, watching her. She turned back to Dean, who stared at the boy, his chest heaving faster. The boy had once been him. Susan realized that somehow, she was witnessing a manifestation from Dean's mind, a reproduction of the child he had once been, a child chained to an unforgettable memory. The child returned Dean's gaze with deep green eyes that cast a looming stare.

"Dean, what happened to you in your childhood? Tell me! There may still be time for me to help you."

Dean turned toward her, his expression crazed, his eyes wide with fear and insanity. He tilted his head back and screamed, unleashing a desperate cry of fear and inescapable terror. The sound of it reverberated through Susan's unconscious mind.

———

RELUCTANTLY, THEY LEFT SUSAN IN HER BEDROOM so they could adjourn and collect themselves. Now having full run of the house, they retired to the living room, exhausted from the episode on the staircase. Dylan focused his attention on the EVP device, hoping it recorded not only the voice, but the flurry of words that erupted from Susan. He began pressing buttons as Leah continued to voice her hesitation.

"I still hate leaving her up there, alone," she said.

"We all hate it, Leah," Brett assured her. "But we can see her clearly on the video monitor. We'll be checking it consistently."

"That's right," Sidney said. "I plan on keeping a vigilant watch over her, all night long if I have to. So, you can get some rest. I'm not at all tired, especially after tonight's events." Sidney had retrieved his glasses from the living room floor below the staircase railing. Fortunately, they remained unbroken.

The EVP device uttered a quick screeching noise, followed by the click of a button.

"We need to carefully listen to this playback," Dylan began.

"The moment when we heard two different voices is crucial. We heard some of those words, but they failed to make sense in the order in which we heard them. I want us to hone our ears as closely as possible. I may have a trick up my sleeve."

Dylan raised the volume, and the racket of earlier background noises crackled through the audio. Then, the spirit's gravel-like voice growled, shouting about how Susan failed to listen when Dean had mentioned the shadows.

"Now she knows," it said. *"You all know."*

Next, they heard Sidney tell Tahoe to step out of the way. Then, after Sidney had asked the question about Dean's childhood, they heard the commotion on the staircase once more.

"I don't know. You tell me, you freak," the spirit cried.

Sidney shrugged and then chuckled. "I've been called worse."

"Pause it right there," Leah said. Dylan paused the recording as she spoke. "Those words prove that Dean never recalled this childhood incident. Whatever it was, it was horrible enough that Dean suppressed it from his memory, as I originally assumed. The anger is a result of either not being able to remember, or the everlasting subconscious mind continuing to deny the event."

"This spirit is trapped in the recurring hell of its own life story which has tragically passed." Tahoe's words lingered for a moment before Dylan resumed the recording.

They listened as Brett continued to coax the spirit. The spirit's response sounded suppressed, restricted. The sound of different voices intertwined.

"I don't—kn—ARRGH! I can't—I can't—Ask—Father—Maguire!"

Dylan paused the recording once again.

"So, who is Father Maguire?" he asked.

Brett was the first to answer. "That's what we have to find out."

"Do you hear how the spirit's words are being interrupted?" Tahoe pointed out. "The dark force of another being is preventing it from speaking freely."

Tahoe's conclusion was accurate. A chill trickled down Dylan's spine. He resumed the recording but fast forwarded through the banter of their voices. Then, Dylan pressed the playback button at precisely the right moment. The cacophony of warped voices mingled together, spewing the stream of words they'd been awaiting.

"Find—kill—her—priest—help—Fools!—me—Elysium."

Dylan stopped the recording, rewound it, and then fast forwarded it, back and forth until the stream of words strung together to make sense.

"Let me see what I can do with this," Brett said. Then, Brett connected the EVP device to his laptop and spliced the words together according to Dylan's demonstration. Then, he created a smaller recording derived from the larger one. "Ready?" he asked.

They listened as two alternating voices spoke.

"Find priest." The spirit's gravelly voice spoke first.

"Kill her." A harsh, warbled voice interrupted.

"Help me." The spirit spoke again.

"Fools!" The malevolent interrupter had addressed them directly.

"Elysium." The last word was a desperate plea.

"Elysium," Sidney noted, "the peaceful realm of the dead."

"It's asking us to help it return there," Tahoe concluded.

"The same voice instructed us to find the priest," Leah said.

"Father Maguire," Brett reminded them. "I'm guessing we need to start searching in Pittsburgh."

"The other voice does not want that to happen." Tahoe's spoke with a grave tone. "It gave the order to kill her—kill Susan. That's what it wants. It sounds like a malevolent force has attached itself to this spirit. The detachment would undo the malevolent, but not if it can kill Susan first."

"In a way, it doesn't make sense." Dylan felt the need to clarify before continuing. "The spirit that called itself Dean wanted revenge over Lydia's death. It mentioned the shadows, which we've already associated with Dean Collier. So, if there are two spirits at work here, then who is who?"

"We cannot know the extent of which the darker force has exhibited its influence," Tahoe answered. "The spirit calling itself Dean may be consumed by unresolved anger, but the darker force is exploiting that anger, using and wielding it as a tool of destruction."

As Dylan resumed the recording again, he heard himself addressing the spirit.

"We're going to find Lauren."

They listened again to the spirit's maniacal laughter.

"No need. Lauren's dead!"

Dylan stopped the recording. Seconds of silence passed. Dark thoughts remained unspoken.

"We need to find out if this is true." Dylan felt a nagging twinge in the pit of his stomach. Tahoe and Leah exchanged solemn glances.

"We'll start in the morning," Sidney said. "We'll track down Lauren. Then, we'll search for Father Maguire."

They sat in somber silence, fearing that in the morning light, the spirit's words would prove to be truthful.

18

THE DREAM OF THE CHIEF

Tahoe took the room next to Susan's as fatigue took its inevitable toll upon him and the rest of the team. Susan remained unconscious, lingering in a sleep laden spell somewhere near comatose. Before surrendering to the night, they prayed over her, but the situation appeared to accelerate. Her color drained to a near stone-white. Spirals of gray had sprouted and streaked her hair in a matter of hours. The malevolence that possessed her was depleting her. Tahoe's heart broke at the sight of it.

Now, he lay awake, staring at the ceiling and listening for sounds coming from the next room, even though Sidney sat inside, keeping watch. Eventually, sleep overcame him, thick and blanketed. Just like the instance a few nights ago, Tahoe's body lay at rest, yet he waded through a plethora of colors. Brilliant gold, orange, red, and magenta combined in an ultra-magnificent sunset. The familiar picturesque desert appeared before him, vast and surreal, and like before, his feet never touched the ground. He'd been here before, only nights ago when he'd met his great-grandfather.

Tahoe turned his head in every direction, exploring the beauty of this majestic landscape with his eyes. Eternal beauty, that's what it was, nothing short of it, a place where death and dying had been vanquished. A place where need had been erased. Something shimmered in the distance. A flash of red and white drew closer and closer as a figure marched across the desert floor toward him. The figure's red and white headdress blew in the desert breeze. In an instant, his great-grandfather, the great chief, stood before him.

"Face to face, once again, Ulisiatsutsa." The chief's tone was stern, grave.

"Great-grandfather, what's happened to me?"

Tahoe referred to the sudden change he felt after confronting the shadows. The feeling of renewed vigor, the rejuvenation of his mind and body, the dreams and instances involving cicadas, and the words spoken by the malevolent spirit, all of it meant something. The chief gazed deeply into his eyes.

"The spirit called you by what you are, Ulisiatsutsa." The chief lifted both hands and rested them on the crown of Tahoe's head. *"Phoenix."*

Tahoe felt a ticklish chill as the chief's hands moved in a feather-like motion down to his shoulders. Tahoe had heard the word before, something about an immortal bird rising up from the ashes, yet another legend of which he'd paid little attention.

"But I don't understand. How and why?"

"In much the same way the malevolent spirit has possessed your friend, I possessed you, Ulisiatsutsa, but only for the time it took to defeat the shadows. I told you, when the time came, I would be there inside you. That is what I meant. Upon that moment, some part of me remained left behind inside you."

"So, you're saying—"

"That you and I have become one to a great extent. You channeled me, and I have touched this world again through you. You and I now coexist."

Over the chief's shoulder, Tahoe witnessed a gathering swarm spread and multiply. The swarm flew forward in a fluttering, tumbling procession, screeching their familiar concerto which grew louder as the swarm widened. The great school of cicadas danced in a flurry around Tahoe, some landing on his shoulder, at his feet, and many flew above his head.

"*The cicadas swarm and pay reverence to whom they deem immortal,*" the chief added.

"But I am not immortal," Tahoe countered. "Such a thing is not possible."

The chief sighed. "*As I have told you before, Ulisiatsutsa, time will reveal all. But right now, time is running out. In regards to your friend, you have assumed correctly. A dark, malevolent force has attached itself to the aimless spirit that possesses her.*"

"So, *there are* two spirits at work!"

The chief nodded. "*The malevolent entity possessed the spirit as a boy. Now, in death, it has claimed the man's tainted soul. The malevolent force seeks to live in the flesh.*"

"Tell me," Tahoe implored. "What can we do?"

"*Your friends must find the old priest. He has fought this malevolence before. He remains experienced and well-versed in threats such as demons and dark spirits. But you all must hurry.*"

"And if we don't find him?"

The chief stared at him somberly. "*Then, your friend will die.*"

The swarm of cicadas flew up and away from Tahoe. The dream was ending. The chief suddenly loomed farther away in a distance that seemed to grow longer.

"Great-grandfather, wait!"

"*You must hurry, Ulisiatsutsa.*" The chief lifted his head up to the multi-colored horizon. "*Time is limited, but through time, all will be revealed.*"

Tahoe awakened in an unfamiliar bed, wrestling himself into an upward position. His heart pounded vigorously. Sweat trickled his forehead. Outside, chirping birds cheerfully greeted the brightening daylight as it crept through the window blinds. Again, Tahoe noticed how fast he planted his feet on the floor and rose from the bed.

Trudging down the staircase, he noticed Leah not far in front of him. She had just left Susan's room. In the dining room, Sidney sat awake, diligently typing and surfing on his laptop.

"I see you haven't slept my friend," Tahoe said.

Sidney turned away from the laptop and met his gaze. "I did for about three hours, but I can't sleep anyway. I'm too wired, too worried about Susan. We have to act fast if we're going to find Lauren and this Father Maguire, if he's even still alive. I've been internet searching for the past half-hour."

"The priest is still alive," Tahoe replied. "Come, I will explain."

Sidney lifted his laptop and followed Tahoe and Leah into the kitchen. There, Brett and Dylan rummaged through Susan's cupboards and refrigerator, scrambling eggs and fixing toast for a quick, makeshift breakfast.

"She looks like she's getting worse, like this thing is killing her." The desperation in Leah's voice was well warranted. "I'm not a nurse or a doctor. I've tried to see inside her with my third eye, but I can't. If she gets any worse, we have to call an ambulance."

Dylan dropped a spatula down in the pan of eggs, and then slung the dishtowel over his shoulder. "And tell them what Leah, that Dr. Susan Logan is possessed? What if she awakens in their custody? We would never get her out of a mental hospital."

"I won't leave her to die in that bed," Leah snapped.

"She's not dying, Little One," Tahoe interrupted. "At least not yet, that's why we must act and move fast. Last night, I dreamed of the chief again." Tahoe told them about the dream, at least the part that involved Susan. "The chief said that we must find the old priest. The priest has already fought this malevolent force that has enslaved Dean's soul." Tahoe informed them of the chief's revelation, that the malevolent entity possessed Dean as a child.

"The childhood incident," Brett concluded. "Dean was possessed by this dark force when he was a boy. That's the secret that Susan never knew."

"*That's* why Lauren assumed that Lydia contacted us," Leah pointed out. "She thought Lydia consulted paranormal investigators about Dean's childhood possession."

"When Lauren realized Susan had no clue what she was talking about, she quickly backed away from us." Sidney's memory remained in sync with Leah's. He kept his eyes on the laptop screen, while vigorously tapping away at the keyboard. "I found her address. That didn't take as long as I expected. Lauren and Eugene Kessler—522 Ashford Drive. They live in a small suburb of Pittsburgh, about ten miles from Lydia's palatial estate."

"It won't take us long to get there," Dylan estimated. "Forty-five minutes, at most."

"Do you think what the spirit said about Lauren could be true?" Brett's question was directed at Tahoe. "Do you think she could be dead?"

Tahoe breathed deeply and closed his eyes. He remembered his earlier vision of Susan and the dark-haired woman in the funeral parlor. He recalled the murky, tainted mist that clung in the air. Tahoe now identified that mist as the malevolent presence. But something else about that earlier vision now disturbed him. The dark haired woman's face and hands had been stained with blood. He felt his heart sink. He sighed before answering.

"That's entirely possible, but some things Leah and I are not meant to see. That's why you must go, quickly."

"Let's hope Lauren is alive and can point us in the direction of this priest," Sidney said. "If he knew Dean as a child, he must be pretty old by now, right?"

Tahoe cleared his throat. "He may not be *that* old, my friend. I'm assuming he's in his early eighties."

Sidney glanced up at Tahoe, wagging his finger at him. "That reminds me, Tahoe. Earlier, the spirit said something cryptic about you. If I remember correctly, it likened you to a phoenix."

Tahoe wondered when they'd get around to asking about that moment on the staircase. Last night, they'd been too preoccupied with Susan. Now, in the morning light, the bits and pieces were being recalled. Tahoe sighed and glanced at their expectant faces, unsure of what to tell them.

"That's right," Brett said. "The spirit claimed it could see inside you, and that you rejuvenate like a phoenix."

Tahoe heard the quick click and clack of plastic keys as Sidney's fingers tapped away again at the keyboard. The laptop screen changed, and Sidney read the words in front of him.

"According to Wikipedia, a phoenix is 'a long-lived mythical bird that cyclically regenerates or is otherwise born again.'"

Tahoe caught the look of concern on Leah's face.

"Is there something you want to tell us, Tahoe?" she asked. "Does this have anything to do with the vision I had of you, surrounded by cicadas?"

Sidney typed the word "cicadas" into the search engine. "Holy shit," he exclaimed. "In mythology, cicadas are said to represent immortality—seriously?" Sidney turned his head, exhibiting a long glance at Tahoe.

"Let's not overreact, my friends," Tahoe said. "Remember, symbolism is a large part of mythology. We are not in mythological times."

Tahoe quickly realized how foolish that last statement sounded after everything they'd witnessed and been through, but it left his mouth before he could stop it. They continued to stare at him, unimpressed.

"So, spill it," Dylan prompted. "What's going on with you? You do seem more alert, more vibrant."

Whatever was happening to him was showing. Others were beginning to notice little things just as he had. The time would come when he would have to explain. Better to let them in on it now and explain to them what little he understood.

"The chief entered my body the night I faced down the shadows. This you all know. That night, something happened to me. In the dream I had last night, the chief confirmed it. I continue to carry the chief's spirit inside me, a direct result of channeling him." Tahoe glanced at Dylan. "You're right about one thing. Lately, I've noticed minor things, like having more vim and vigor, a physical burst of energy I haven't felt since my forties. These past few days, I've been able to accomplish minor tasks with much less effort than before. My arthritic pain has all but ceased. But as to the exact reason for all this, I remain unsure. Once again, the chief advised me that time would reveal all things, and all things will be answered, yet that does little for our investigative minds, now doesn't it?"

"So, you mean you're getting younger?" Sidney blurted out the question with a burst of sophomoric enthusiasm.

"How is that possible, young ones?" Tahoe laughed, but secretly, he sensed something inside him mocking his laughter. "No matter what, I'm eighty-years-old. I believe what's happening is the result of a spiritual resin left behind in my body. We spoke of this before. Remember, the chief was somewhere in his fifties when he died, an age I have long surpassed."

"And you think this burst of vitality you've experienced is a part of the chief's soul lingering inside you?" Brett asked.

Tahoe nodded. "It is the best and most logical explanation."

"Since when have we dealt in logic?" Leah's adamant tone persisted. "I don't think we really know what logic is because for us, both logic and reason have flown out the window together. I know what I saw in my vision. I saw you surrounded by cicadas. It was a message."

Again, Tahoe sighed. "But there is no need to dwell on it now, Little One. We have far more pressing matters at hand. If we don't find the old priest, Susan will die. That I know." He turned to Sidney and Dylan. "What are you both waiting for? You have Lauren's address. Go, find her and the priest. Brett, Leah, and I will remain here."

"I've discovered a couple of hits on the name Father Maguire, of Pittsburgh." Sidney rose from the chair as he spoke. "We may have to start searching if it turns out that Lauren—"

"Don't say it, Sidney," Leah advised. "Just go, and hurry."

19

A MURDER-SUICIDE

"You drive the van." Sidney tossed the keys to Dylan as they plodded down Susan's walkway. "I need to follow up on these few hits I got from the internet." Sidney had printed out his research results on Susan's printer. Now, he held the sheet of paper in front of him in the van's passenger's seat, eyeing it carefully. Dylan started up the van and drove away.

"It says here that a Father Patrick Maguire once served at the Holy Patronage Church in Pittsburgh from 1960 until 1968." Sidney read from the sheet in front of him. "That would've been around the time he'd known Dean Collier, at least according to Dean's age at the time Susan treated him. Dean would have been a boy in the sixties. Then, I discovered an article from 1980 about the same priest, whose charity work with needy children was widely documented."

"Has to be the same priest," Dylan guessed. "How many priests with the same name from the same area have a calling for helping children?"

"The church he served back then was the Saint Jude's Cathedral in Hillview, about forty-miles north of Pittsburgh."

"So, he moved." Dylan assembled the pieces of information like a puzzle as he drove. "If we have to track him down in Hillview, we've got a long day ahead of us."

"Yeah, but I'm hoping this priest is still alive as Tahoe claimed. He has to be at least eighty-something. What if he's too old to help us? What if he's moved on from there and lives somewhere else?"

"Let's not get ahead of ourselves. Let's find Lauren first."

After forty-five minutes, Sidney entered the bustling city of Pittsburgh for the second time in less than a week. Pittsburgh, the place where three rivers met below skyscrapers and clipper ships sailed slowly in the midst of it all, the place where geographically, he and the team pinpointed as home. But this time the van's GPS guided him and Dylan in a different direction, more to the east, toward a relatively quiet, residential section.

"I think I've been to this part of the city before," Dylan observed. Suddenly, he pointed to a line representing a street on the GPS display. "Ashford Drive is two blocks away. We're close." Dylan continued to deliberate the best way to handle the meeting with Lauren, mentioning how it was obviously a difficult time for her, but they had to tell her the truth about what was going on, no matter how crazy it sounded.

"I doubt she'll dismiss us," Sidney said. "I saw how curious she was when she thought we knew about Dean's childhood incident. When we tell her what we know, we'll be getting our feet in the door. She'll talk to us then. I know it."

A dull beeping sound droned from the GPS. "We're here," Dylan announced.

Sidney paid attention to the houses, glancing one by one at their numbers as the van passed. He turned his head away for a moment. Flashing red and blue lights mingled with the orange glare of morning sunshine, catching his attention. Outside of 422 Ashford Drive, Sidney counted three cop cars and two ambulances idling in the daylight. Suddenly, he felt his insides turn to stone.

"Oh, no." The dread in Dylan's tone served as silent

confirmation of the spirit's foreboding words, yet Sidney said nothing.

Dylan slowed the van, edging as close as possible to the two-story, maroon-brick structure numbered 422. Two male officers stood on the front lawn, talking, while a young female officer stood at the end of the driveway, waving Dylan to either move forward, or park on the opposite side of the street.

"Something awful has happened," Sidney declared. "She's posted there, redirecting passing onlookers. There must've been quite a few already."

"Those two ambulances are not moving. Not a good sign." Dylan glanced in the rearview mirror, back at the female officer, and then to the curb on the opposite side of the street. "We have to find out what's happened. It's urgent. I don't care if we look nosy or suspicious, let them arrest us."

Dylan parked the van between two cars, and then keyed off the ignition. The officers stood watching.

"Since I'm the one who actually met Lauren," Sidney advised. "Let me lead the conversation. Just agree with everything I say."

Dylan eyed Sidney closely. "Normally, that would be a pretty scary thought, but okay."

They exited the van, slamming the doors shut behind them. Sidney noticed the two male officers studying them as they approached the female officer.

"Officer," Sidney began, stepping cautiously toward her. "My name is Sidney Pratt. I'm a friend of Mrs. Kessler's. Can I ask what's going on here?"

The female officer, whose long black hair was slicked back into ponytail, leaned in closer to hear him better. "What did you say your name was again?"

Sidney repeated his name and introduced Dylan. "I just saw Mrs. Kessler yesterday at her daughter's funeral viewing. We were wondering if she was okay."

The officer closed her eyes and shook her head. "I'm afraid not, guys."

She glanced over her shoulder, nodding to her two male colleagues, who then turned their attentions away. One of them spoke into his shoulder mic. Then, the same officer began to direct the EMT's out of the house. Two of them pushed a gurney toting a black body bag. Behind them, another gurney carrying a second body bag lingered.

"My God, is that Lauren?" Sidney cried.

"Shh, listen, guys." The officer held out her hands to Sidney. "I'm not going to lie to you. It's not good. I'm afraid you can't stay here. Right now, this is an ongoing investigation, so there's not much more I can tell you. I'm sorry, but you can't help your friend now. So please, the Press is on their way here. We can't turn this into a spectacle."

"Officer, I assure you, we're not the Press," Dylan said. "Is there *anything* else you can tell us about our friend?"

She shook her head.

"You said you saw her, yesterday?" she asked Sidney. "You may be asked a few questions somewhere down the line as they try to reconstruct yesterday's events. They may want to speak to everyone who had contact with her, so I'll be keeping your name, Mr. Pratt."

Sidney agreed, simply nodding as the sounds around him suddenly died away, leaving him deaf as a stone. His clairaudience had taken over, yet he tried to maintain his composure in front of the female officer who now simply stared at him. Inexplicably, his focus was directed toward the male officer on the lawn who spoke into his shoulder mic. He stood a considerable distance away, but Sidney heard his words, loud and clear through the deafness.

"Coroner's calling it a murder-suicide. Looks like the wife did the husband in, and then herself."

Then, crashing static followed.

"Roger that," a voice responded. *"Ten-four."*

Sidney shook his head, a reflexive attempt to rid himself of the deafness, yet it already passed. Chirping birds resumed in the background. Baffled, the female officer continued to stare at him, somehow silently realizing that Sidney had a knack for something, something she couldn't understand.

"Come on, Dylan, let's go." Sidney turned and crossed the street back toward the van. He stopped, turned, and noticed Dylan lingering. The female officer stood silently, at a loss for words. "Come on, let's go!" Sidney called out in a testy voice. Dylan thanked the officer and followed Sidney back to the van.

"What just happened, Sid?" Dylan started the ignition and took off down the street.

"My clairaudience seems to be taking on a different form," he said. "This is the second time, as of recently, that I've heard remotely. I stood there as the deafness occurred, and I heard that cop talking into his mic. It was a murder-suicide. I heard him say that the wife did the husband in."

"I knew it—two gurneys and two body bags."

"The spirit was telling the truth," Sidney surmised. "Lauren is dead."

"Her husband too, by the looks of it."

"It killed her. It possessed her and killed them both. We have to hurry, or it's going to kill Susan and possibly the others."

"Then we have to find the priest, which means we have a two-hour drive ahead of us, but first, we have to call and warn them. Their lives are in danger."

20

TRAPPED

When Sidney called, Leah pressed the speakerphone button so that Brett and Tahoe could hear. As Sidney spoke, Leah's third eye showed her visions depicting his words. She saw Lauren standing crookedly, staring up at the ceiling, her face fixed in a twisted sneer. Invaded by the unseen malevolence, Lauren stood stricken, possessed, like Susan. Leah's third eye roved like a moving camera, revealing a gun cabinet, and then a drawer just beneath. Lauren smashed the cabinet's glass and took a pistol from the drawer, opened a door, and fired upon her husband. Leah flinched, envisioning his body jerking backward by the force of the bullet. Through her closed eyes, Leah watched as Lauren's hand rotated and then pointed the pistol up to her head. Fire, blood, and then Leah's eyes opened wide.

Sidney's voice continued to blare through the speakerphone. "We saw them removing the bodies. I stood listening when the deafness took over. I know what I heard."

"You heard correctly, Sidney," Leah said. "I'm seeing it all as you speak. You're right. It possessed her. Where are you now?"

"Just outside of Pittsburgh, on our way to Hillview," Dylan interjected. "We're off to find this priest on our own." A silent pause ensued. "We don't need to tell you how impertinent this is now. Pray that we find this man, and that we're back in time."

Tahoe sat adjacent to Leah in Susan's living room. He chimed in to the conference call.

"He is there to be found, my friends. This I have been told. May God's hand lead you to him and bring you back in time. Godspeed."

"We should arrive in Hillview in about two hours," Sidney added. He promised to keep her posted and advised her to call him immediately if Susan's condition changed. Leah agreed.

"The spirit wasn't taunting us." Leah pressed the end call button and set her phone back down on the coffee table. "It killed Lauren in the most heinous way. I saw it. I saw her pointing the gun to her head. Through Lauren, the spirit mimicked Dean's suicide."

"Ironic, isn't it?" Brett observed. "I've locked Susan's gun back in its box and stashed it in the trunk of my car. I figured we'll all be safer without that thing lying around the house."

Leah sat watching the laptop, studying the video footage of Susan's bedroom.

"Look, something's happening." She called out to Brett, who hurriedly sat down next to her on the couch. Tahoe joined them on the other end. They watched a decimated Susan twist and writhe in her unconsciousness, trapped in an inescapable nightmare.

"It looks like she's fighting it," Brett said.

"Let's go upstairs and attend to her, lest she break the bonds that bind her."

Tahoe's suggestion made them rise from the couch and quickly ascend the stairs together. Opening Susan's bedroom door, the feverish stench of sweat and sickness swept them. Susan's upper body tossed and turned, back and forth. Her legs kicked futilely, making a swooshing noise against the sheets. The leather belts creaked in response.

"Susan." Leah spoke gently, resting the palm of her hand against Susan's forehead. Susan suddenly stopped fidgeting and lay motionless beneath Leah's cool touch. A tear streaked Leah's cheek. "Susan, can you hear me? Don't let it win. Remember that you're a fighter. Come back to us. We're here waiting for you."

Susan's expression suddenly changed. A forming frown framed a look of worry on her sleeping face.

"Something's taking place right now, wherever she is," Tahoe declared. "I can feel it."

———

DEAN'S TERROR-FILLED SCREAM SHOOK HER AND echoed like thunder. The sound of it plunged Susan back into the pitch black sea. Now, she felt herself fighting to be free of it, yet no amount of thrashing ended the darkness or brought Dean back. A sudden coolness touched her and calmed her. Then, like before, a sliver of light penetrated the blackness and slowly overwhelmed it. Again, she was back in her office at Meadowbrook. Dean lay on the couch, his eyes wide and affixed to the ceiling in fright.

The thoughts absorbing her now were those of the psychiatrist she'd always been. Instinctively, she sat behind her desk and kept her eyes focused on him. His chest rose up and down. Careful not to alarm him, she asked the question, and this time, she listened.

"Dean, what were you about to tell me the last time we met?" She watched his lips quiver and his eyes grow wide. "It's alright, Dean. We're safe here."

Dean expelled a gasp. "None of this has been my doing, Susan. It was inside me when I was a boy. The shadows brought it back." His breath heaved harder and raspier. "It wasn't me who pulled the trigger. It possessed me, like it possesses you now."

Susan felt an icy chill. Dean's words began to make sense.

"So, the malevolence is not you?"

Dean sat up, shook his head, and responded.

"I sought my way into everlasting oblivion, but the shadows had awakened me and the malevolent in the process. This faceless thing tried to claim my soul as a child and failed. Now, it has claimed it in death. I'm trapped by it, and now so are you."

"But it spoke angry words over Lydia's death. I heard it."

"I felt anger, Susan, something I shouldn't have felt if my soul were at rest. The malevolent attached itself to my soul and used the grief and anger I felt watching Lydia die. It used it like a weapon. I should be at rest, but it won't leave me."

Bits and pieces fell together in Susan's mind. She remembered what she hadn't before, the doppelganger, the possession, the wolf, and then walking up the stairs. She rose up from her chair and placed her hands down on her desk.

"So it's trapped us here." Susan hissed in angry determination. "Well, I'm not going to let it get me, Dean, and I promise I am finally going to do right by you. I'm going to end this for you, once and for all. I'm about to stake my life on it."

21

FATHER MAGUIRE

THE DRIVE NORTHBOUND TO HILLVIEW TOOK A LITTLE over two hours, just as Dylan had estimated. After making it far from the city, they traveled through rural woodlands for miles until reaching the quaint, historical town, where street meters continued to ring out in antiquity. The town appeared small and quiet, and set snugly against a backdrop that seemingly never changed. Between the internet directions Sidney obtained, and the van's GPS, it hadn't taken them long to find Saint Jude's Cathedral just off of Baker Street. Dylan noticed the cathedral was much smaller than most, yet its red and blue stained glass windows and various outdoor statues made it none-the less spectacular. Dylan parked the van in the side parking lot.

"Let's pray that if this priest is no longer here, someone can lead us in his direction," he said, turning off the van's ignition.

Sidney scoffed. "You can blame my parents for my usual lack of faith or interest, but right now, I'll try anything." Sidney crossed himself. "Not that anyone will hear *me*."

They exited the van and walked to the front of the cathedral. After pulling its heavy doors open, they stepped inside. Standing in the cathedral's hallway, they noticed just ahead of them, how a long strip of maroon carpeting made a great pathway through the church part, becoming an aisle that separated rows of pews on the left and right. At the end of the aisle, a golden altar stood horizontally, and behind it, a crucified Christ hung from a massive wooden cross on the wall. The smell of wood polish wafted in the air around them. The church sat empty, the afternoon sun glaring through its stained glass windows. To their left, down the long hallway, were various rooms.

"Come on, let's check it out," Sidney said. "See if we can find anyone around."

They walked down the hallway, passing rest rooms and a room with a closed door. Then, at the end of the hallway, light emanated through a half-closed door. The clacking sound of fingers tapping away at a keyboard became louder as they walked farther. The room at the very end of the hallway was an office. Dylan knocked on the door, and after a slight pause, a woman's voice told him to come in. Dylan and Sidney stepped inside.

A gaunt woman in her sixties sat behind a desk, her typing paused by the knock at the door. She glanced at them with a somewhat surprised expression and asked how she might help them. Dylan began by introducing himself and Sidney.

"We're looking for Father Patrick Maguire. I believe he served here some years ago."

Now, the look of surprise on the woman's face appeared warranted.

"You're right," she said. "Father Maguire hasn't been here in years. He retired in 1998."

First, Sidney apologized for the interruption. Then, he fell in step with the first order of discretion the team usually maintained.

"We come bearing sad news about a friend of his. Maybe her name rings a bell, Lauren Kessler? Father Maguire may have known her as Lauren Collier."

Dylan interrupted. "Do you know how we might contact Father Maguire? It may be better if we told him ourselves."

The woman appeared hesitant. "Like I said, Father Maguire

hasn't been here in years. But if you want to leave a message with me, perhaps I might be able to get it to him."

"Listen, Miss—" Sidney prompted.

"Ridgley," the woman answered. "Iris Ridgley."

"Miss Ridgley, here's the truth. We're paranormal investigators who've traveled a very long way to see Father Maguire." Sidney blatantly abandoned the first order of discretion. "We're dealing with a case of possession, demonic or otherwise, and we heard that Father Maguire could help us."

The woman's eyes grew wide. "Say no more. Please sit down." She motioned them toward two chairs opposite her desk. Dylan and Sidney sat across from her. "I was Father Maguire's secretary for over twenty-five years. I'm well aware of his history with this type of thing." Iris leaned in closer to them and lowered her voice. "Although through the years, Father Maguire has exorcised the upmost discretion because of the Church's disdain and reluctance over such issues."

Dylan explained that he was the paranormal team's chief-investigator, and the possession case in question dealt with Dean Collier, a boy Father Maguire once helped.

"The name sounds familiar, but it may be a little before my time with him," Iris said. "Father Maguire didn't always talk about the cases he worked on, but I did help him document a few in the following years."

"You see, a dear friend of ours is the victim," Sidney explained. "If we don't get help quick, we're afraid we may lose her, forever."

Iris began writing something on a memo pad. When she finished, she tore off the sheet and handed it to Sidney.

"That's Father Maguire's address," she said. "He lives in the rectory a half-mile down the road. It's not far from here. I'll call ahead and tell him to expect you both."

"Iris, I can't thank you enough," Dylan said, rising from his chair and shaking her hand. "You've saved us a great deal of time."

"And hopefully, our friend's life." Sidney also shook her hand, calling her help invaluable.

"I'll be praying for you both, and especially your friend," she said. "May God bless and protect you both, and everyone involved."

Dylan and Sidney thanked her one last time before leaving the cathedral. Within minutes, Dylan fired up the ignition and sped away.

———

THE ELDERLY FATHER MAGUIRE'S HAND SHOOK AS HE hung up the phone. His former secretary, Iris, phoned him and mentioned a name he hadn't heard in years, a name he never thought he'd hear again—Dean Collier. Iris described two young men, paranormal investigators, who arrived at the cathedral in search of him.

"Very polite young men, said they had sad news about someone named Lauren Kessler, formerly Collier. They were adamant that it was in regards to a boy you encountered years ago, a possession case named Dean Collier. They seemed to desperately need your help. I didn't know what else to do."

"Not to worry, Iris," he said. "You did the right thing. They're for real, all right. They wouldn't know about Dean Collier unless they were."

Now, with great unease, he sat remembering. Dean was the boy of two parishioners he befriended way back in the late sixties. He'd been a young priest around thirty-years-old at the time, but discretely well versed and experienced in both demonic and malevolent forces. He'd encountered it early, having seen such things in other parts of the world when he was still a missionary, places such as Haiti, the Dominican Republic, Mexico, and here in the United States. Dean had always attended mass with his parents. Father Maguire remembered what a friendly, likeable boy he'd been. When Dean's parents, Doris and Henry, came to him for help they were desperate, almost grief-stricken although the boy hadn't died. They'd heard of his endeavors as a missionary and as a priest. Turning them down was not an option.

Luckily for the Colliers, Dean had not been possessed by a demon, but a boundless malevolent entity. Demons sought to take the souls of the living to Hell with them, whereas malevolent spirits blindly sought to invade and live in human form, regardless of the cost to the victim. They lacked the strength and determination of demons and often failed out of an inherent sense of confusion. Through patience, love, persistence, and the power of Christ, he'd driven the malevolent from the young boy. Later, Dean would not remember one moment of the incident, and it was never spoken of again. He and the Colliers continued on, as if nothing happened, yet they all remained watchful over the boy. Eventually, he moved, yet Doris and Henry always knew where to find him.

Then, one day about twenty years ago, he received a letter in the mail from Lauren Collier. She explained that she was Dean's wife, and even though Dean still did not recall the childhood incident, Doris and Henry had told her the entire story. The letter's author wanted to know more, wanted to know if she and her daughter were safe. Would the malevolent force ever return? Could it possess her innocent little girl? She'd even asked the most important question that Doris and Henry had pondered for years. What could have caused the malevolent manifestation in the first place?

Who knew the answer to such things? Certainly, he never pretended to know the inner workings of the divine or the supernatural. All he had was a certain insight, a sound knowledge, and his trust in God and all things good. Each time he'd faced a possession case, he prayed hard that his efforts would prevail, yet they hadn't always. Like the twelve-year-old boy in Haiti.

The case had later reminded him of Dean Collier. He'd been a young missionary and an apprentice to Father Halloran, an elder priest who traveled the world in his missions. He studied diligently under his leadership. A young peasant girl, a seer of some type, claimed to have seen a dingy, yellowish-brown-colored mist surround and seep into the boy. Then, the boy became violently possessed by it. The boy raged, physically striking out at others and flinging his head and body into wild twists and turns, while bearing the wide whites of his eyes.

Father Maguire had helped Father Halloran try to exorcise the spirit from the boy. The young, clairvoyant peasant girl was the boy's neighbor and babysitter. Father Halloran allowed her to be present, a rare and unusual concurrence. In the thralls of the exorcism, the girl cried out, pointing and claiming to see the mist as it left the boy's body. But it was too late. The boy died on the soiled bed of his ransacked bedroom. The spirit had drained everything from his small, youthful body. Unlike the Haitian boy, Dean Collier had survived, but not entirely.

He heard about Dean Collier's suicide back in the nineties. The tragedy occurred not long after he received his wife's letter. Had the malevolence returned to reclaim Dean in his adult life? Father Maguire wondered if that's actually what was happening at the time he received the letter. If so, could the malevolent force have been drawn to Dean by some type of attraction, almost like a magnet? Father Halloran had explained to him that the Haitian boy was not possessed by a demon, but a malevolent entity, as he called it. The question of why remained. Father Maguire guessed that something about the Haitian boy and Dean Collier attracted the malevolent forces, but the identity of that something remained a mystery, and yet another question he failed to answer.

How helpless the Collier boy had been, strapped to his bed like a wild animal. Father Maguire still remembered the curses hurled at him by the rough, gravelly voice that did not belong to the boy, the feral calls of the soulless abhorrence that dared to inhabit a child. Fifty years had passed, but those memories remained forever etched into his mind. At eighty-years-of-age, he recalled the images perfectly, as if they'd occurred only recently.

After the Collier incident, he participated in two more separate possession cases, both victims having fallen under demonic persuasion. One of those cases occurred here in western Pennsylvania in 1978, the other in New Hampshire in 1983. Father Maguire was glad to never witness another possession case since then, but now on this day, far away in his eightieth year, he sensed that the blissful quiet was about to be shattered.

———

THE RECTORY WAS A SMALL RESIDENTIAL-HOUSING village situated a half-mile down the road from the cathedral, just as Iris Ridgley described it. Small dormitory-style buildings housing retired clergy members sat side-by-side amid quiet, peaceful surroundings. Father Maguire resided in Redemption Hall, and Dylan drove slowly until arriving at the sign perched on its front lawn. After parking the van, they trudged up a small set of stairs to the porch. Suddenly, the front door opened, and an elderly man with white hair and glasses stepped outside to greet them. He stood, a short man, wearing not the traditional priest's garb and collar, but a tan-colored sweater over a dress shirt with pants. He lifted his head slightly and gazed upward at them through his bi-focal lenses.

"Excuse me, Sir," Sidney began. "We're looking for Father Patrick Maguire."

"You found him." The short elderly man's answer was quick and focused.

"Father Maguire, we're so glad to find you." Dylan introduced himself as the chief-investigator of the Paranormal Research and Investigative Society from Green Valley University, and then introduced Sidney. "I realize you don't know us, but we can prove who we are." Dylan removed his driver's license, as well as his university ID from his wallet and handed them to the priest. Sidney did the same. Dylan continued. "I'm also a professor at the university, as was my father. They can vouch for both of us. I'm afraid something horrible has happened. That's why we're here. We need your help desperately."

The priest lowered his eyes, sighed, and then glanced back up at them. "Iris informed me of the nature of your visit." He motioned to the door with his hand. "Come inside."

They stepped into what appeared to be a house equipped with a living room, a vast dining room, a kitchen in back, and a staircase that no doubt led to bedrooms and bathrooms. Father Maguire opened a side door in the kitchen and led them through a hallway, and to a room at the end. They entered a small office, furnished with all the typical office needs. Seeing a desktop computer in the elderly priest's working quarter's surprised Sidney, but there it was. The same type of chairs in Iris Ridgley's office aligned the back wall. Father Maguire pointed to them.

"Gentlemen, if you don't mind grabbing two chairs."

They both took a chair from the back wall and situated them in front of the priest's desk. Father Maguire sat behind his desk, stretched his arms out, and then folded them so his elbows pointed down upon his green-felt blotter. He stared at them expectantly, his eyes peeping just above his glasses. Sidney felt momentarily flabbergasted, unsure of where to begin. Dylan's silence somehow echoed his predicament. Father Maguire broke the awkward hush.

"You mentioned a name to Iris, one I haven't heard in decades. In fact, the last time I heard that name was before either of you were born, I'm sure."

"Dean Collier." Sidney realized that as far as the priest was concerned, that was the beginning, and that's where he would start. "Father, the reason we're here is because our friend's life depends on it. We wouldn't have ventured all the way here from Green Valley, if it weren't a matter of life and death. Our friend, Susan Logan, is the director of our research society. She is also a psychiatrist. To be more precise, she was Dean Collier's psychiatrist at the Meadowbrook Institution in the 1990's."

Dylan picked up the story, explaining how Susan was fired after being accused of misdiagnosing Dean. "Dean committed suicide shortly thereafter."

Father Maguire nodded.

"During the course of our last investigation," Sidney continued, "Susan was reminded of Dean through a somewhat ghostly encounter."

Sidney thought it pointless to divulge details about the shadows. The society's cases were primarily confidential, and he failed to see how the shadows bore any relevance to Father Maguire. The clock was ticking, and there was no time for anything but the bare facts.

"In order to understand what happened after that, you must know that among our small team is one of the world's most renowned psychics, Tahoe Manoa. Tahoe's clairvoyant third eye is regarded as one of the most powerful in the world. Shortly after our last case, Tahoe experienced a vision of what he called, a 'sickly, yellowish-brown haze' surrounding Susan."

Sidney's words sparked Father Maguire's attention. The old priest flinched, and then leaned forward, his eyes glued to Sidney's.

"A malevolent," he said.

"That's correct, Father," Dylan replied. "This malevolent spirit eventually made its presence known to us. It referred to itself as 'Dean.' We then assumed that Dean Collier was the malevolent spirit, hell bent, as they say, on vengeance against Susan."

"But we were wrong," Sidney pointed out. "When I asked the spirit what happened to Dean in his childhood, it reacted violently. That's when it spoke your name. It told us to ask Father Maguire."

The priest's eyes widened.

"So, you only know of me because the spirit mentioned me?"

"We even recorded it, Father." Dylan assured him, referring to the shoulder bag he'd brought with him that contained the EVP device.

"It was Tahoe who concluded that Dean was possessed by this malevolence as a boy," Sidney continued. "Then, once the spirit spoke in alternating voices, we realized that the malevolent was not actually Dean Collier but the entity that once possessed him. It has since attached itself to him in death."

Father Maguire's eyes grew even wider, and then closed in silent prayer. He made the sign of the cross, and that's when Sidney realized the priest was startled by the notion of a malevolent entity imprisoning someone's soul after death. When Father Maguire opened his eyes, Dylan removed the EVP device from his shoulder bag.

"Father, if you'd like to hear it, I can play it back for you," he offered.

Father Maguire stared at the EVP device, his index finger resting across his lips as he pondered. He lowered his finger, and then interlocked all of them together in an astute manner. "Let's hear it."

Dylan pressed a button, and once again, he and Sidney listened to the spirit's ramblings on the staircase. Father Maguire's expression remained stoic and unchanged even as he heard his own name being called out. He listened to the warped words and the incitation to "find the priest." Then, the spirit proclaimed its cryptic announcement that Lauren was dead. As the recording ended, Dylan pressed the stop button and waited for the priest to speak. Father Maguire calmly removed his glasses, folded them, and set them down in front of him, a cool, composed, and well-played performance at concealing his shock. He stared at them gravely.

"Iris said you had sad news regarding Lauren Kessler." The priest paused. "Is she dead?"

"Yes, Father." Sidney said the words as gently as possible.

Father Maguire closed his eyes again and sighed, lifting his hands together in silent prayer. When he finished, Sidney told him about how they'd looked up Lauren's address in order to find her and warn her.

"We also thought she might be able to help in locating you, Father," Dylan told him. "But when we arrived at her house, the police had taken it over as a crime scene."

"They're treating it as a murder-suicide," Sidney said. "I managed to overhear the officers talking." Sidney figured he wasn't actually lying to a priest. He *did* hear what was said. Telling the priest about his clairaudience was another unnecessary burden bearing the issue of relevance. Besides, overloading this man whose help they desperately sought was not a good move. "Apparently, Lauren Kessler killed her husband, and then herself."

"But as you can hear from the recording, Father," Dylan explained, "the spirit warned us that it had already taken place. This malevolent force possessed Lauren and used her body for its murderous rage. What's worse, as I'm sure you understand, is that this recording will never stand up in a court of law. No one will believe what really happened."

"And naturally, Father, they won't believe Susan is possessed by a malevolent entity. They'll label her as a shrink who descended into madness, and the end result will be her death. You may be our only hope of getting her back."

Sidney felt a tinge of hope as Father Maguire nodded his head. Then, Dylan made a proposal.

"Father, we realize you don't know us, so we understand if you want to verify our identities and credentials first. But if you would come back to Green Valley with us, I will handle all your expenses and accommodations. You have my word that we'll bring you back here as soon as this nightmare is over, whatever the end result may be."

Sidney heard Dylan's voice quiver slightly. Then, Dylan swallowed hard, trying not to let his emotions through to the surface. It was yet another indicator to Sidney as to just how real this whole thing was, and how rapidly it all occurred. Sidney studied the old priest's face as a silent pause ensued. His nerves twitched, waiting for the priest's answer.

"Can you give me thirty minutes?"

Sidney's heart leapt. The feeling of relief intensified, but so did a restless frenzy brought about by a figurative and unseen hourglass.

"Father Maguire, we don't know how to ever thank you." The only words Sidney could muster gushed out in a wave of relief.

"Don't thank me yet," the priest replied. "The malevolence has yet to be undone. I would just like to make something clear. It's been almost forty years since I involved myself in this sort of thing. When something like this happens, there are no guarantees. There are no definite outcomes, no certainties. I will do my best to save your friend, but ultimately that's up to God."

The priest sighed, put his glasses back on, and continued.

"In my younger years, I witnessed and soon became involved in exorcisms quite by accident. My mentor, a priest named Father Halloran, had secretly worked in this area, that is to say, without the church's permission and most likely against their wishes. You see, in the past, the church has always been reluctant and unmoved toward this sort of thing. Oddly enough, they do not always believe. Rules, regulations, and stipulations exist regarding exorcism, not to mention that one must present an almost unreachable burden of proof to sustain one's claim that another is possessed. The church usually rules against the execution of such practices. Only once have I conducted an exorcism with the church's holy sanction. All other instances, such as the case of Dean Collier, I have participated in without the church's knowledge or permission. So, I understand your need for discretion and secrecy, but I assure you, it goes both ways."

"Understood, Father," Dylan reassured him. "All our cases are confidential. We'll keep your name out of our records, Father. That's not a problem."

Father Maguire needed time to quickly prepare and bring everything he might need.

"I'm old," he continued. "I suspect this will be my last endeavor of this nature. Let's hope so, anyway. I do this not only for your friend, and the fact that I am so called forth, but I think of Doris and Henry, long gone. I think of their helpless little boy strapped to a bed, a slave to a faceless malevolence he'd attracted by some innocent encounter. I do it for the boy that in his subconscious mind, never really got past what he failed to remember. Let's pray that God will be with us."

Sidney hadn't actually prayed since childhood. Sure, when the team came together often in prayer, he bowed his head respectfully and conformed. But he hadn't really prayed in a long time. Now, he bowed his head and seriously prayed. Father Maguire asked for God's protection on the journey back and during the exorcism. He prayed for Susan and for the passage of Dean's spirit into a peaceful eternity.

"Amen." The three of them uttered the word in unison.

"I'll see you both back here in thirty minutes. I'll be ready and waiting at the door."

Father Maguire suggested a small diner not far down the road, where they could grab a quick cup of coffee. Sidney and Dylan thanked him again, vowing to return shortly. On the way out, Sidney stopped at the door and turned back to face the priest.

"Could you say one more prayer, Father?" he asked. "Pray we make it back to Green Valley in time."

————

THROUGH THE SHEER CURTAIN OF A SIDE WINDOW, Father Maguire watched Sidney and Dylan get back into the van and drive away. Earlier, he'd tried not to show his shock in front of them. Between what they'd told him, and the voice he heard on the EVP recording, he knew one thing for certain. This type of malevolent had gained a strength and power unparalleled to anything he'd ever experienced before in his vocation. His training as a priest had taught him to disavow any beliefs in hocus-pocus phenomena such as EVP's, yet secretly, he'd always known better. He'd witnessed and experienced too much over the years to entertain such denial. Listening to that thing call out his name on the recording, he'd remained still and expressionless, yet his heart had skipped several beats.

This malevolent force not only infiltrated the human body yet again, but it had done so freely, committing a double-homicide as a test of its strength. The malevolent had built up energy and amassed strength through its own volition, proof that it was ruled by conscious, evil forethought. Its goal was clear, to inhabit a physical body for as long as possible, in hopes to one day master the act of possession. He wondered if such a thing was possible. Could such an unholy infection honestly befall the human race?

He shook himself out of the dark momentary reverie. He couldn't allow such thoughts to distract him. Today, out of nowhere came the call to confront an evil he hadn't faced in years. The two young men were right about two voices intertwining in the recording. He'd heard it himself. "Find the priest" had sounded like a call for help. It could have also been a vengeful ploy, the angry spirit's chance to lure him back into the turmoil, but he couldn't be certain.

He shuffled up the stairs to his room, where he unzipped an overnight bag and stuffed some clothing inside. Then, he opened a dresser drawer and retrieved his thick, black Bible. He closed the drawer and opened another, this time bringing a sliver crucifix up to his lips and kissing it in reverence. Digging into the back of the drawer, he retrieved a purple-velvet pouch. Inside were two small vials, one containing blessed holy water, the other containing a sanctioned mixture of oil and salt. He placed the Bible, the crucifix, and the pouch inside a briefcase, and then changed into his black garb and collar. It was necessary for what he was about to do.

Back downstairs, he stood at the front door waiting, his heart pounding. He closed his eyes and prayed for peace and strength. Soon, the white van appeared again in front of Redemption Hall. It was time to go. Evil had called him back into the fold. Now, he would answer that call, once and for all.

22

CHILD'S PLAY

SOMEWHERE IN THIS DARK, SHADOWY OBLIVION, SHE and Dean remained trapped. Somehow, Susan temporarily adjourned all thoughts of her untimely death. She wasn't so convinced that her death had actually occurred; not if what Dean said was true, that the malevolent force had taken possession of her body.

She stood with her hands placed down upon her desk, having just sworn to Dean that she would do right by him. As he sat on her office couch, his head turned to the left, espying something or someone in the wavering darkness. She turned her head also, gazing in the same direction and recognizing an image as it slowly developed.

Once again, the image of Dean as a boy stood in the shadowy dimness, but this time, the boy held something in his arms, something Susan couldn't make out. Fear struck the Dean who sat on her couch. He heaved and gasped, threatened by the image of the boy he had once been.

"It's only an image Dean, a ghost of the past," Susan assured him. "He cannot hurt you. Watch the boy, Dean." Her voice grew louder. "He has something to show us."

Susan stepped closer to the image, hoping to gain a better view. The boy held what appeared to be a rectangular game board. While holding it to his chest, the boy hunkered down on his hands and knees, and then placed the board in front of him. Susan took tiny steps, inching herself closer in order to see what the boy played with, yet careful not to frighten the ghostly specter away. Glancing upside down at the board, she saw letters in rows, depictions of the sun and the moon, and the words "Yes" and "No."

A Ouija board. The boy was playing with a Ouija board. Behind her, Dean's heaving turned to sobs and moans.

"It's over now, Dean." She spoke to him softly, her voice caressing. "It's all in the past."

Slowly, the sounds of his anxiety subsided. Susan stood fixedly, witnessing the wooden planchette move right and left as it spelled out letters the boy scrambled to piece together. Her eyes moved along with the planchette, taking note of the chosen letters.

D-O-O-R

"Door," the boy said.

That word had been easy enough for the boy. Susan paid close attention to the next round of chosen letters.

L-E-T-M-E-I-N

In her mind, Susan separated the letters to make words.

LET ME IN.

A missing piece of the puzzle had just fallen into place. The ghostly boy stood up from the ground, turned, and walked toward a door that grew faintly visible.

"No!" Dean cried out from the couch. "No, No, NO!"

The boy opened the door, admitting a burst of sunshine that made him squint. He stood seeing no one, yet something malevolent passed through the doorway.

———

EYES THAT BELONGED TO SUSAN LOGAN FLINCHED OPEN

and wide, casting a glare at the camera situated just above the bedpost. Susan's body writhed with the spirit's anger, thrashing and violently contorting in futile attempts to break the bonds. The spirit growled from within her, clenching and gnashing Susan's near perfect teeth. Again, the spirit mustered all of the strength it learned to wield and project, but now, that same strength felt weakened by the human flesh and the bonds that restricted it, tamed by the body's cage that now confined it. The spirit raised Susan's upper body as far as possible and scowled once again at the camera. After collapsing backward, the spirit manipulated Susan's hands, yanking harder to break free of the leather belts. The squawking sound of leather stretching meant the bonds were slowly loosening. Then, the spirit let out an unearthly scream that echoed off the walls and through the house.

———

AFTER HOURS OF SILENCE AND FRANTIC IDLENESS, LEAH received another update on speakerphone from Sidney. Just as the chief foretold, Sidney and Dylan had located the priest. They now sat in a diner somewhere in Hillview. Tahoe, Brett, and Leah listened intently. Sidney told them about finding Father Maguire in the rectory. He'd agreed to return to Green Valley with them. They were picking him up in twenty minutes.

"We should be back in two and a half hours," Sidney estimated. He asked about Susan.

"There's no change," Leah reported. "Although she looks like she's fading away."

"You know, I prayed earlier in the rectory," Sidney said. "For the first time in many years, I prayed." He paused. "I'm going to keep praying."

"You've done well, my friends." Tahoe felt a small inkling of hope he would keep to himself. The chief had predicted that unless Sidney and Dylan found the priest, Susan would die. They found the priest and were soon returning. "Drive safely. You've done your part. Now, all is in God's hands."

As Leah ended the call, a scream, deep and hollow yet booming, traveled from the upper floor and down to the living room with a resounding echo. Tahoe shivered at the sound of it, like the call of the damned or the scream of a banshee. They hurried over to the laptop. Susan's body writhed on the bed, her head jerking wildly, her hands yanking the bonds in captive fury. Then, the writhing and screaming suddenly stopped. The whites of Susan's eyes peered through almond-shaped ovals at the camera.

"We've got to get up there, now." Brett turned away from the laptop and ran up the staircase. Leah and Tahoe followed behind him. As Brett turned the knob and swung the bedroom door open, the three of them barreled inside.

Susan's upper body slumped back down on the bed. Then, her head lifted up and plopped down repeatedly on the pillow. Tahoe could almost feel what was happening.

"It's becoming restless." He raised his voice in an effort to admonish the spirit. "It's aware that it is losing this fight. Something unexplainable has weakened its presence."

"Go to Hell, old man!" The voice wailed in a rough, scratchy warble. "Die!" The voice subsided into a growl.

"You are neither dead, nor alive," Tahoe said. "Go back to where you came!"

Susan's hands yanked again at the leather belts and failed to break them. Infuriated, the spirit lifted Susan's upper body again and spit at the three of them.

In a moment of blind anger, Leah reached out to grab Susan's face, yet Brett stopped her.

"It's still Susan, remember that," Brett said, holding her back.

"Why don't you leave her?" Leah screamed.

The maniacal laughter they'd heard on the staircase erupted again. The laugh eerily fluctuated between three different tones. Then, the laughter segued into a menacing growl. The spirit cursed and threatened through clenched teeth.

"When I break these bonds, I'm going to kill you bastards! ALL OF YOU!"

Anger, an emotion Tahoe hadn't felt since his youth, overcame him suddenly. It combined with the sense of helplessness he felt standing over Susan, unable to help her as he'd helped Brett and Leah in the past. He stood fuming, feeling powerless as the malevolent voice echoed through the room, inflicting terror upon their souls.

———

SIDNEY AND DYLAN KNEW THAT AN AWKWARD SILENCE would fill the van during the ride back to Green Valley, and how right they'd been. Obviously, Father Maguire was no stranger to the supernatural and paranormal happenings of this world, those unexplainable elements from an unseen realm that often crossed heinously into this one. He'd even hinted that his lengthy experience with possession cases began long before either of them was born. Father Maguire carried with him a history, so Sidney and Dylan decided in the diner that they would reveal to him the basic aspects of who they were as a team. Sidney decided the moment was now, before the silence became unbearable.

"Father, before you embark upon your mission, I felt you should know more about us," he began. Sidney turned backward from the front seat to face him as Dylan drove. "The members of our team, including myself, are specifically driven to paranormal investigations because of who we are as people." He paused. "What I'm trying to say is that each one us has some unique psychic talent that we've inherited at birth or has experienced and endured some paranormal instance that has shaped us as investigators. Earlier, I mentioned Tahoe Manoa, the clairvoyant among us. However, there is another."

Sidney described Leah to Father Maguire, and how Tahoe encountered her when she was a child. He talked about how Leah, as a child, witnessed demons in Cedar Manor and later wrote a book about it.

"'Cedar Manor' was the title," Sidney explained. Father Maguire narrowed his eyes, as though the story or the title sounded vaguely familiar. "We later conducted an investigation inside the house. Then, there's me," Sidney continued. "I'm somewhat of an opposite of Leah and Tahoe. I'm known as a clairaudient. I don't see things. I hear things, including the dead. Now Father, I don't mean to hit you with all this, and I don't expect you to believe. It's not a requirement. But I felt we owed it to you to be up front about who we are."

"And I appreciate your honesty." Father Maguire thanked him. "But after all I've witnessed in my life, I wonder if disbelief is even possible. You know, Sidney, the Bible tells of many instances in which the living heard the dead speak, King Solomon among them. Don't expect me to disbelieve you just because I'm a priest. I'm also an old man who has seen many things, things of which I can only offer up speculative explanations as to the reasons why."

"Then hopefully you'll understand, Father," Dylan said. "Because there's more to us than what Sidney has just told you, so much more. We are the paranormal investigators surrounding the mass UFO sighting in Green Valley. I was directly involved in the incident, having experienced an apparent abduction I can't fully remember."

Dylan made eye contact with Father Maguire in the rearview mirror. The priest stared at him, shaking his finger.

"I thought you looked familiar," he said. "Now I know from where. I remember seeing the incident on the news and in all the papers."

"That's right. Our friend, Susan, has been trying to help me regain my memory of that night, but all I've recovered are images, bits and pieces of a puzzle I can't quite assemble perfectly. I suppose that in some way I'll always be haunted by that night."

"I'll pray for you, Dylan," he said. "But I'll also pray for Susan because of what will take place this evening. You know, I've always wondered what it was that enticed a malevolent being or a demon to take possession of a human. For errant spirits, I always suspected it was an attraction of some kind. But there is one thing that both spirits and demons have in common, and that is that sometimes they are lured by an unwitting invitation on the part of the person who becomes possessed." Father Maguire told them about his past cases, specifically, the Haitian boy. "I later learned of a rumor that the clairvoyant girl was involved in voodoo. It's a popular and common practice in that part of the world. She was said to have involved the boy in her rituals. Of course, Father Halloran and I hadn't known that at the time. I realize you all assumed this spirit was that of Dean Collier, but could it be possible that Susan inadvertently extended an invitation of some kind during the course of your investigations?"

The next part of the discussion Sidney had been hoping to avoid. Psychic investigators were one thing, but Sidney thought it was best to circumvent the details of the Black Mirror and Susan's doppelganger. But the truth remained unavoidable.

"Susan has been through Hell this past year, Father, literally," Sidney replied. "It began with a case that presented itself to us not long after the UFO incident. We investigated a black mirror once used by a satanic practitioner. It had become a cursed occult object before disappearing for many years. Susan located the mirror, and then became consumed by it."

Sidney told the story of the Black Mirror, and how Susan's doppelganger emerged from its hidden gateway. Then, Father Maguire listened intently as Dylan described the whirlwind turmoil that enrapt Susan as a result of her mischievous double.

"For months we tried to find her," he said. "But with no luck. Then, there she was in Susan's house, living with her, dwelling in invisible silence."

"They say Abe Lincoln once saw his doppelganger," the priest said. "As I told you, there isn't much I will dismiss."

Sidney described how the malevolent spirit had possessed Susan's doppelganger.

"Yes, of course," Father Maguire concluded. "That would explain my attraction theory. The spirit was attracted to the doppelganger because it suspected she wasn't human. It had to discover what she was. It may have also been fooled by her. When that failed, it turned its attention toward its real target, Susan. But I'm not going to lie to you both. I don't believe I have to tell you what you're dealing with here. This malevolence has not only infested and possessed, but it has controlled and manipulated physically. It has committed the ultimate sin wearing the skin of a human. If it is the same spirit that once possessed Dean, it has now taken control of his soul and is using it to gain its strength. It's like a virus that continues to grow more infectious and uncontainable."

Sidney's nerves fluttered at the priest's words. Quiet devastation filled the van.

"So, you're saying there's no hope for Susan?" Sidney needed to know now.

"I didn't say that. But what I am saying is that this malevolent force is strong, and its intent, I'm afraid, is to kill. It's already shown that. I don't suspect its intentions toward your Susan are any different than its wrath against Lauren. You said you didn't pray often, Sidney. I would start now."

Sidney sat quietly startled by a sudden rumble of thunder. A flash of lightning streaked across the sky. Dylan's windshield wipers squeaked back and forth as a torrential downpour pounded the van's hood. Then, Dylan broke the calming quiet.

"I just thought of something. You said that those possessed have often extended an unwitting invitation, like the Haitian boy who was involved in the voodoo rituals. Do you think that could have been the case with Dean Collier? As a boy, did he participate in some innocent form of child's play that invited this malevolent into his life?"

Father Maguire sighed. "I could never be sure. Naturally, his parents were baffled over the incident. But one day, after I pressed Doris, she told me she found a Ouija board in the hall closet about a month before the incident. She swore she had no idea how it got there. She'd immediately gotten rid of the board, but never thought anything of it. I never knew if that was the whole story, and with so little to go on, I could never conclude with any certainty that the Ouija was the cause."

"Well, whatever the case was, Dean's life was certainly beleaguered by paranormal entities." Sidney decided to tell Father Maguire everything. They were now more than an hour away from Green Valley. Better that he knew everything before going into Susan's house. Sidney couldn't risk Susan's life by not sharing all pertinent information. "I'm afraid there's more to this story, Father, but you should know everything. I don't want you to think we're keeping anything from you. Less than a week ago, Father, we encountered entities we originally assumed were demonic in nature, but they weren't demons. They were shadows."

Sidney told him about Tahoe's experience with the shadows, and how they'd followed him back to Green Valley. He detailed how the case connected to Dean, and how Lydia had given Susan a video cassette.

"The video seemed like a suicide farewell." Dylan spoke to fill in the blanks. "In it, Dean mentions being haunted by these shadows. We've concluded that they are the reason for his hysteria and eventual suicide. We also suspect that they caused the death of Dean's daughter, Lydia, and awakened Dean's restless spirit."

"And that restless spirit brought with it the malevolent that attached itself to it." Father Maguire correctly surmised the point.

Lightning flickered across the sky as another crash of thunder split the silence. Before long, the familiar sights of Green Valley emerged through the rain-soaked windshield. Within ten minutes, Dylan swerved the van through the spiraling maze of King's Haven. Susan's house appeared just as they left it, but now the outside lights were turned on in anticipation of their return. The storm continued as they walked up the stairs to the front porch. Sidney noticed the front door opening, and there stood Leah, holding the screen door open and ushering them inside.

"Everyone, this is Father Patrick Maguire." Sidney began the introductions. "Father, this is Leah Leeds."

Leah shook the priest's hand and thanked him for coming. "I'm afraid that what's happening now, Father, is far beyond our expertise. We were unsure of where to turn."

"As I told your friends, I pray that I can help, but what you all are facing is a dangerous malevolent force."

Sidney introduced Father Maguire to Tahoe, and then to Brett.

"As I mentioned, Father, we all have our own unique experience with the paranormal," Sidney said. "If there's time, I'm sure Brett can fill you in on his story."

Brett chuckled lightly under his breath as Sidney winked at him.

"I'm mainly the chief computer-technician of the team, Father," Brett said. "I'm sure you'll be interested in what we've set up here." Brett led Father Maguire over to the coffee table where the laptop was set up. "We had quite the uproar within these past few hours. Tahoe seems to think something's changed, as if the spirit is weakening."

Father Maguire stared at the screen, examining the footage of the sleeping woman. All appeared to be docile and quiet. Then, the malevolent force inside her opened her eyes.

23

AN EXORCISM

FATHER MAGUIRE DREW BACK FROM THE SCREEN. THE malevolent eyes stared straight at the camera and through to his soul, almost as if they had been expecting him. He'd sensed a dark, unholy presence when he stepped through the door. Now, he was absolutely certain of it. Glancing at these five paranormal investigators, he also sensed an obscurity that clung to them, one they immersed themselves in rather than abandoning. Though they were good people, they poked and prodded, pursued and dabbled. Clairvoyants, clairaudients, a claim of alien abduction, and another young man whose story had not yet unfolded, it came as no surprise that as the young woman claimed, they'd now encountered something beyond their callings.

This clairvoyant named Tahoe Manoa struck his curiosity the most. Who was this man? Father Maguire felt something unexplainable while standing in his presence. Native-American by heritage, Tahoe had to be his age or near enough, yet he exuded some type of youthful quality, one Father Maguire couldn't quite pinpoint. The man's hair was definitely gray, yet black strands appeared to force themselves through the grayness. How odd for a man his age.

Father Maguire glanced at the screen one more time. The possessed woman laughed softly through closed lips, her chin wobbling up and down in steady silent gaiety. He turned back to the five anxious faces awaiting his response.

"Take me to her, now," he said. Earlier, he collected everything he needed and carried it along in a black briefcase. While examining the screen, he'd set the briefcase down for a moment. Now, he picked it back up off the floor. "I'm as ready as I'll ever be."

The investigators escorted him to the staircase. Leah led the way up the stairs, and then slowly opened the door to Susan's bedroom. Leah and Tahoe entered first, followed by Sidney, Brett, and Dylan. Father Maguire prayed for a quick moment, blessing the doorway in front of him. Then, he entered. He felt heat in this room, not a normal furnace heat, but an unnatural rolling wave of sickness and tension.

Father Maguire stepped closer to the bed and looked down on the woman who lay as a confined prisoner upon it. Her feet and wrists were bound by leather straps, belts apparently. A beautiful face for a woman of her age, somewhere in her late-sixties, he guessed. But now that face appeared drawn and withered, her complexion a deathly pale, as if the malevolent spirit inside her drained every drop of life from her body and soul. Fresh spirals of gray hair sprouted from the bottle-colored blonde mass she obviously kept consistent. Her friends made a circle around the bed, keeping vigilant watch over her. Father Maguire could see the love they had for her. He sensed the maternal bond she shared with the younger ones, and the great friendship that existed between her and Tahoe. They would do anything to save her, and apparently, he, an elderly priest, bore the distinction of being their last hope.

Susan's eyes widened, exposing glossy, dilated orbs that glared fixedly at him.

"Well," Father Maguire began. "You called out my name, or at least one of you did." Abruptly, the spirit writhed inside Susan, twisting her body and uttering a low guttural growl. He'd chosen his words carefully, calling out the spirit for its hijacking of a restless soul. The growling grew louder, the sound of an angry dog provoked by a hasty human hand. He stood stoic and undeterred. "What is it you want with this poor woman? She's done nothing to you." He paused, ready for the reaction to his next words. "And neither has Dean, not in life, and certainly not in death."

Susan's upper body reeled forward. The spirit's coarse, guttural growl segued into a hellish scream. Both a male and a female voice combined together in a warped cacophony.

"You son of a bitch!" the spirit screamed. "I'll leave your dead carcass for the vultures to feed upon!"

"It is you who will soon exit, malevolent one, not me!"

Just then, Father Maguire stopped as he heard a creaking sound. Those surrounding the bed exchanged glances. Upon further inspection, they noticed that Susan's hands were twisting, attempting to break the leather bonds that secured them.

"She's going to break the bonds!" Brett yelled.

As Brett reached over to grasp Susan's struggling hand, a loud snap cracked from the side of the bed. The thin leather belt restraining Susan's left wrist broke under a fierce gathering strength. Before Brett could grab a hold of Susan's free arm, her clenched fist swung clockwise and socked Father Maguire in his right eye. He stumbled backward, but Dylan quickly steadied him, breaking his near fall. Dylan, Sidney, and Leah quickly ushered him out of the room, but not before he caught a glimpse of Brett and Tahoe struggling to keep Susan restrained.

A splitting crack of thunder rumbled outside, eerily competing with the warped screaming that continued in the bedroom. Dylan and Sidney whisked him into the upstairs bathroom. Leah ran to the small kitchenette on the second floor and quickly returned with an ice pack.

"I'm alright, really," he protested.

"Father, we are so sorry about this," Dylan said

"Don't apologize," he said. "This is a fight that's been going on longer than any of you have been alive. Please, get my briefcase. I left it behind in the bedroom."

As Dylan turned, Tahoe appeared in the doorway, holding the briefcase. Father Maguire thanked him and then addressed Tahoe's earlier conclusion.

"You're right, Tahoe," he said. "Regardless of that virulent display of physical strength, the malevolence inside her is growing weaker. It is failing. It is angry, but it is also becoming desperate and vindictive. The time to drive it out is now or never. The more we wait, the greater the chance it will claim her body, her life, and her soul."

Father Maguire took the briefcase from Tahoe, the contents of which would be crucial for what was about to happen next. He felt a sting as he removed the ice pack from his eye and handed it to Leah. The slight swelling around his right eye proved to be minor.

"Again, Father, we're so sorry about this," Leah offered.

"Don't worry about the eye, my dear." He laughed. "A small price to pay for all the things I've seen in my life." He gazed at them with a more serious expression. "Now, it's time to go back in there."

———

ONE BY ONE, THEY VENTURED BACK INTO SUSAN'S bedroom, with Father Maguire trailing behind them. Once inside, the investigators stood side by side, blocking the angry spirit's view of Father Maguire, who laid his briefcase down upon Susan's bureau and opened it. He retrieved the two vials from inside the purple-velvet pouch and clutched them in his left hand. Then, with his right hand, he lifted the crucifix up to his forehead and made the sign of the cross. Removing the Bible from his briefcase, he opened it to where it had been bookmarked. He read the words quickly, yet there was no need. The words were forever etched upon his heart and mind.

He turned and walked toward the bed, reciting the Lord's

Prayer as he did. The investigators spread out and surrounded the bed, allowing him sole space at the foot of it. The restless spirit inside Susan flailed her head from side to side, emitting a low growling noise on the verge of roaring fury. At the end of the Lord's Prayer, all hearts and voices proclaimed "Amen."

Then, the spirit mocked them with its maniacal laughter, unleashing an unending, repetitive cackle that sounded almost mechanical, as if it drew no breath while taunting them. Father Maguire was reminded of its long ago performance, its sinister antics when it took over the soul of Dean as a boy. This moment also made him remember the incident in Mexico. A young woman in her twenties had been possessed by a malevolent force that tried to act as a demon, yet he and Father Halloran knew well the difference. Father Maguire had recognized the signs of a witch. "Bruha," the locals had called the young woman. She had inadvertently let something in. Father Maguire drove the spirit out of the young woman that day. She had lived to tell the tale.

Now, he spoke a prayer in Latin, and then flung the holy water in thin sheets over Susan's body. The spirit writhed, attempting to break the bonds once again. It was losing its strength, but still, it fought on. It laughed again.

"Water, Father, mere water." The voice remained a warped twisting of male and female inflexions. "Is that all you have?"

"Not by a long shot." Father Maguire began to recite the Prayer of Saint Michael the Archangel. *"Most glorious Prince of the Heavenly Armies, Saint Michael the Archangel, defend us in our battle against principalities and powers, against the rulers of this world of darkness, against the spirits of wickedness in high places. Come to the assistance of men whom God has created in His likeness and whom He has redeemed at a great price from the tyranny of the devil."*

Father Maguire took the second vial containing the mixture of oil and salt, the one Father Halloran had given him many years ago. He used it several times over the years. Now, the last of it remained in his hands. He flung its contents over Susan's body, causing a more violent reaction than before. The spirit screamed in torturous pain, wrenching Susan's hands and feet in futile attempts to break the leather restraints.

"OW! I'LL TEAR YOUR SOUL TO PIECES YOU PHONY BASTARD!"

Susan's face flushed with the spirit's seething fury. Bloodshot eyes glared at him. Nostrils flared. Susan's head and body shook with uncontrollable tremors.

"Why don't you tell them what you've been hiding all these years, Father?" The voice roared solely with its rough male inflexion. "Why don't you tell them you're just like them?"

Father Maguire remembered what happened after he'd driven the malevolent from the Mexican woman. Father Halloran had taken him aside and handed him the purple-velvet pouch.

"I want you to take this," he said. "Keep it for as long as you live. Hopefully, you will never have to use it all. It is the blessed oil and salt of the exorcism. You, my young priest, have the natural ability to drive out the forces of evil. How or why I do not question, but God has given you a unique gift. May the Lord God be with you, always."

Father Maguire had never told a soul about his mentor's words. Now, this angry, vindictive malevolence sought to expose him. He felt their eyes upon him. He flung the oil and salt over Susan's body again. The scream echoed through the room, resonating deep down into their souls.

"You came into this world through a doorway opened by an unsuspecting child, you coward!" Father Maguire flung the contents of the vial once more. "I cast you back into the realm of darkness, back through the doorway you once stepped through!"

Susan's body pivoted into an upward arch. Only the whites of her eyes glared up at the ceiling. Her lips drew wide apart, locked in an ongoing scream.

———

THE GHOSTLY REALM THEY REMAINED TRAPPED IN

shook with seismic-like tremors after the boy opened the door. Then, Susan saw it clearly, the yellowish-brown mist that seeped through the doorway. Unwittingly, the boy Dean had not only welcomed, but ushered the malevolent entity into his life. The boy hadn't realized what he'd done; he was too young to understand. Now, still sitting on Susan's office couch in this ghostly setting, Dean understood. The vision of the past had shown him what he'd done. When it began to make sense, he'd cried out, hoping the vision would stop.

As the sickly-colored mist hung in the atmosphere, Susan saw a chance. She promised Dean she would do right by him, and if the slightest possibility of correcting the past existed, she had to take advantage of it. Perhaps it was the reason they were now locked together in this unexplainable hell. Maybe if she acted now, they could both move on. The mist continued to hover, making its way toward the boy.

Susan ran toward the boy, grabbed him by the wrist, and whisked him out of the way. She stood underneath the strange mist, watching it hover and rest, and realizing that the mist was no ordinary plume, but an evil, malevolent consciousness, faceless and without a form, waiting to inhabit. Susan bent down, picked the Ouija board up off the ground, and gripped it firmly in her hands. She gazed into the mist.

"Come on," she said. "You know it's not the boy you want. It's not Dean." She nudged her head sideways to Dean, who sat watching. "You can't do anything with him. You can't live inside him. He's dead! It's me you want, isn't it?" The mist descended lower and closer to her. "That's right, it's me you want now, otherwise, I wouldn't be here."

She had to be alive; she felt her heart beating. Turning her head slightly to the left, she noticed that the ghostly door through which the mist had entered remained open. She stepped slowly, inching herself sideways toward it.

"You want me?" She screamed. "Come and get me!"

Susan turned and ran through the doorway, the board clutched firmly in her hands. On the other side, dim light flickered everywhere, offering quick glimpses of unfamiliar surroundings. She moved as if underwater. Glancing behind her, the yellowish-brown mist followed and now chased her through an indefinite world. Ahead, through the flickering light, she saw three doors. The doors were opening, and slamming shut of their own accord. Susan stopped, realizing her attempts to catch her breath made the realm around her all the more real. She watched the doors open, slam shut, and open again, unsure of which one to enter.

The mist surrounded her. Susan remembered there was someone who could hear her.

"Sidney! Sidney, help me!" She screamed again, but realized that even if Sidney somehow heard her, there was little he could do. The choices stood in front of her. The choices were hers. Something about the first door told her not to enter. The third door somehow felt like a trap. The second door, the one in the middle somehow invited her. Unexplainably, the second door was her first instinct, her first choice. Susan felt as if she had nothing left to lose. Her intention was to save Dean from the malevolence that now began to cloud her vision with its murky mist. Now was the moment, right or wrong. Susan ran through the second door, and it slammed behind her. She continued to run, until once again, she swam through an infinite blackness.

———

THE SPIRIT'S ONGOING SCREAM SUDDENLY STOPPED. IN the quick passing of an instant, Sidney's world fell silent. He stood over Susan's bed, waiting and listening through the deafness.

"Sidney! Sidney, help me!"

"She's there!" He spoke, deaf to the sound of his own voice. "She's calling me."

Sidney heard doors slamming, just as the shadows had predicted. Then, sound returned. Father Maguire's voice cried out in Latin, stark admonitions to leave the afflicted. Susan lay unresponsive, her mouth gaping open in what looked like a silent scream.

Father Maguire stopped.

"Oh, God! No!" Leah's voice shattered the sudden silence.

"NO!" Sidney cried out. "No, she can't be. She can't be!"

Brett acted quickly, wedging his body inward. He tilted Susan's head back slightly, pinched her nose shut, and after covering her mouth with his lips, administered CPR. Coming up for more air, he interlocked the fingers of both hands, creating a butterfly pattern, and then placed them on her chest. He administered chest compressions. Then, Brett locked his mouth on hers again, breathing rapidly, and continuing to pump her chest. He repeated his actions, but Susan's lifeless form lay unresponsive on the bed, her complexion waning. Brett breathed into her open mouth again. Nothing.

"NO!" Sidney screamed.

"Susan!" Leah called out.

Dylan ran his fingers through his thick hair. Tahoe looked on gravely.

Abruptly, Susan heaved, gasped, and choked for air. Her eyes opened, and her chest heaved violently.

"That's it, Susan, breathe!" Brett called out to her. "Breathe, damn it!"

Tears shed, and prayers of relief echoed throughout the room. Father Maguire made the sign of the cross and offered prayers of thanks. Wheezing and rasping, Susan continued to breathe.

"Leah, I should've listened to you," Sidney cried. "Call 911."

24

OUT OF THE BLACKNESS

LIGHT CUT SLOWLY THROUGH THE BLACKNESS. THE images above her remained blurry, people she knew, a room she knew well. The familiar voices fought for attention: Sidney, Brett, Leah, Dylan. Brett carried her down the staircase. Then, the red flashing lights roused her fully awake. An ambulance. She was being rushed inside on a gurney. Brett and Leah climbed inside the ambulance just before it sped away.

It all happened so fast, rushing her into a triage unit in the ER, poking her, prodding her, taking her blood pressure, and affixing an oxygen mask over the lower part of her face. She became more and more lucid as the fresh air filled her mind and body. She hadn't been able to speak well; her throat remained dry, her vocal chords weak. But she heard every word Leah and Brett told them.

"She'd been fighting some kind of a bug for some time now," Leah maintained. "We kept telling her to see a doctor, but you know how doctors make the worst patients."

"When we couldn't get a hold of her," Brett said, "we rushed over to her house and found her unconscious. That's when I performed CPR."

Susan recognized their patented cover stories. Something

happened, but what, she had yet to remember. She recognized the young intern in the white coat standing over her temporary bed. He was new at the hospital, young and eager to learn. No doubt Leah and Brett could convince him of just about anything.

"Luckily you did," the young intern said. "If you hadn't, she might be dead right now. It looks like you got her here just in time."

Susan glanced at Leah and Brett, knowing she had to follow their lead, for they had much to tell her. The final diagnosis was that she was severely dehydrated after suffering a spell caused by her low-blood-sugar level. Susan did suffer from a touch of hypoglycemia, though she knew damn well that was not what happened.

"You, of all people, know you could've ended up in a coma, Dr. Logan," the intern insisted. "You're very stubborn and very lucky."

Now, they moved her into her own room and finally gave her water. Suddenly, her room seemed crowded. Dylan, Sidney, and Tahoe arrived, bringing with them a man she'd never seen before, a priest. As she stared at him quizzically, Sidney introduced him.

"Susan, this is Father Patrick Maguire. This is the priest who saved your life."

"I'm afraid I can't take the credit." Father Maguire took her hand and patted it. "Your friends saved your life, especially this young man here." He turned to Brett. "His breath is what brought you back to this world."

Susan remained unsure of what happened. She glanced at each of them, puzzled. After a brief pause, Sidney spoke first.

"It possessed you, Susan. The spirit turned its attention toward you after it failed to possess 'her,' your doppelganger."

Susan suddenly remembered. Her doppelganger blackmailed them. Then, the malevolent spirit possessed her. They watched her demise, right in Susan's living room. Susan remembered walking up the staircase. Then, her mind went blank.

"At the top of the stairs," she said. "That's the last thing I recall."

"That's the moment it took possession of you." Dylan described the incidents on the staircase, her bouts of unconsciousness, and how they'd restrained her to the bed. "We recorded most of what happened on the staircase. The spirit inside, whether it was Dean or the malevolent entity, told us to find Father Maguire, so we did. We drove to Hillview and brought him back here. Regardless of what he says, we wouldn't have you back if not for him."

Susan thanked Father Maguire as a tear streaked down her cheek. Together, they prayed, and he said a blessing over her. Afterward, Susan had a question.

"You said, whether it was Dean, or the malevolent entity. I think I know what you mean." Susan hadn't been clear on what happened before the world went black, but she remembered every moment of the blackness: meeting Dean in her office, the boy, and vowing to Dean that she would do right by him. She remembered thinking she was dead. She told them of the vision she recalled clearly, how the boy had unwittingly let the malevolent force inside. "Dean let it through the doorway when he was a child. He didn't know." She told them about the Ouija board and how the spirit coaxed the boy to let it in.

"I knew it," Father Maguire said. "I knew it all along."

"All of it was so real," Susan reflected. "Just like the blue realm." She detailed how she diverted the malevolent spirit away from Dean and the boy. "Somehow a duality of Dean Collier existed, the man and the boy. The malevolent spirit possessed both of them, but I knew it had to possess something living. Dean could not see that. I knew it needed me, so I let it chase after me. I remember plunging into the pitch blackness yet again. Then, the next thing I knew, I was choking for air, and you all were standing over me."

"You'll never know the relief we felt, hearing you choke," Sidney quipped.

"We honestly thought you were dead," Leah told her.

Tahoe stepped closer to her bed. "As there is much to tell you, I had a reason for maintaining hope to the very end, and here you are. But maintaining hope was difficult in the face of what we experienced. You're a true fighter, my friend."

Susan thanked him, all the while keeping her gaze affixed to his face. Something was different about Tahoe. His face looked tighter. Even his hair seemed less gray. She quickly turned her attention back to the discussion.

"Now when I think of Dean, there's a peaceful feeling inside me," she said. "I feel as though he's finally moved on. I feel like I helped get him there."

"Somehow, I think you're right, Susan." Father Maguire gave thanks once again.

Finally, Susan assured them for the fifth time that she was okay.

"I'll be out of here in twenty-four hours. Watch and see. Now, please, go lock up my house."

Once the room cleared, she lay in her hospital bed thinking of the past year. How close she'd come to danger, not once, but twice, all because she chose to investigate the Black Mirror on her own. What relief she felt now in this quiet moment. She no longer had to worry about her doppelganger, and memories of Dean Collier lay forever at rest in the past. Dean had moved on; she had done right by him. Yet she knew this quiet moment to be only temporary. Tahoe mentioned having much to tell her. The team would wait until she was discharged, and then tell her everything they would not say here in the hospital. She shuddered at the thought of what they hadn't yet told her. A small part of her considered letting the investigators do their jobs, and she would oversee their future cases from the director's chair. After the past year, she could use some time on the sidelines. Susan reclined back in the bed, anxious to get back to normal, whatever that was.

––––––––

THE CONFUSION THE SPIRIT FELT SUDDENLY VANISHED,

gone with the strange-colored mist. Dean knew who he was, who he'd been. He left this world long ago, but the malevolence had sought to stop him from moving on. Susan kept her word; she'd freed him of the evil force that bound him for so long. Now, he felt peace as the blackness disappeared and the confines of Susan's office with it. Light burst everywhere around him. A deep serenity filled his soul. Through the light, a figure walked toward him, a benevolent being with waves of long red curls. His beautiful daughter, Lydia, extended her hand, and they walked home together.

25

LINGERING MYSTERIES

THE EXORCISM LEFT FATHER MAGUIRE BOTH physically and emotionally drained. Trying hard not to show it, the evening's events rendered him wobbly on his feet. Dylan reserved a room for him at a small local inn, more of the Bed and Breakfast variety, as Father Maguire had insisted on something quaint, something more along the lines of his custom. Besides, it was only an overnight stay.

Outside, the storm passed away, curtailing into a constant drizzle that would hopefully clear by morning. He sat awake in the late hours, marveling at what had just occurred within the space of a day. Today, he'd planned on attending a local charity auxiliary luncheon, where he would've discussed church fundraising issues. Instead, he'd been whisked away by two paranormal investigators, one of them part of a psychic trio, to confront a malevolent entity he'd faced nearly fifty-years ago. Sure enough, it was the same evil force that had taken control of an innocent boy all those years ago. He'd been educated as a man of God, a scholar of the Scriptures, yet that didn't stop the chill that gripped him from head to toe, thinking about how such a dark entity managed to sustain itself for many years, feeding off the soul of one who it eventually claimed. The malevolent force had amassed strength so powerful that it achieved life in the physical, long enough to commit two horrendous murders.

In the morning, Dylan and Sidney joined him at the inn for breakfast. Afterward, they went back to the hospital, so he could pay one last goodbye to Susan, who thanked him yet again. In less than twelve hours, she appeared more lucid and vital. A healthy complexion now colored her face with life. He felt an inner burst of joy and relief as he looked at her.

"If you ever need me for any reason," he said, handing his card to her.

"I am forever in your debt, Father," Susan said.

He said his goodbyes to each of them. He shook hands with Tahoe, still unable to discern why a much younger spirit exuded from this elderly man. The man's smiling face made him appear even younger. Then, Father Maguire shook hands with Brett.

"You're a brave young man, Brett," he said. "Someday, you must tell me your story."

Brett laughed. "I'll do that, Father, but I warn you, one surprise at a time."

This time, the long drive back to Hillview proved to be a quiet, yet peaceful ride. As the van pulled up to the rectory, Sidney opened the door and let him out.

"I'll be praying for you, Dylan, and that someday you remember," Father Maguire said. "I'll be praying for all of you."

He turned and ascended the stairs in front of the rectory.

"By the way, Father." Sidney called after him. He turned and faced him. "Is it true, what the spirit said? Are you just like us?"

Father Maguire wondered when that question would arise. He stood and thought for a moment.

"Yes, Sidney," he nodded. "I suppose I am."

With a wink of his right eye, he turned and walked back into the rectory.

———

SOUL SHARER. TAHOE HAD HEARD THAT PHRASE OFTEN throughout his life but never imagined it would one day apply to him. After dinner this evening, he and Brett quickly researched the subject online. Brett found an interesting article about how when two beings share souls, it results in a give and take. The taking, on the part of the living being, results in a great energy, a mass rejuvenation of the physical body and the soul. Rejuvenation, immortality, the message delivered by the cicadas. Tahoe now shared the soul of his great-grandfather, the warrior chief. Phoenix, the chief had called him, like the bird that rises from the ashes in rejuvenation. In Tahoe's case, he was rising from the gray ashes of age.

Inside the farmhouse, he stood staring in the bathroom mirror as Brett suggested.

"Go and see for yourself," he said.

Tahoe stood in disbelief. His now sharpened vision noticed how the wrinkles under his eyes nearly vanished. His skin had somehow tightened, making him appear somewhere his early sixties, but that was not all. The natural black hue of his hair seemed to be replacing the graying whiteness he'd earned as an old man.

Just then, Brett opened the bathroom door. "See, what did I tell you?"

"You're right, my friend. It appears that Sidney guessed correctly. By some oddity, I am becoming younger."

Tahoe thought about returning to Arizona and having to explain what was happening to him to those who knew him. How would he ever explain? Besides, if this was real, he would prefer to stay with those who really understood him. After all, he and the team were now connected in more ways than one. Outside of a few distant great-nieces and nephews, the team had become his only real family. Brett had extended an offer to live with him, here at the farmhouse. His returning home would only raise unwanted attention and questions. If this was really happening, he needed to be here with them, where they could observe and study what was happening to him. And Brett was right, of course. At first, Tahoe thought of being too old to live alone, but now, all that seemed to be changing in front of his eyes. He looked at Brett standing in the doorway.

"I've decided to stay," Tahoe said. "I think it's wisest, at least for now."

"Good," Brett replied. "How do you feel?"

Two words entered Tahoe's mind—rejuvenation—immortality.

———

NIGHT DESCENDED ONCE AGAIN OVER GREEN VALLEY. Exhausted by the past forty-eight hours, Dylan fell fast into a deep sleep long before midnight. As sleep took him over, so did the dream. He stood once again atop Eagle Rock Mountain. The UFO's bright green lights engulfed him. Then, his bare back touched a cold metal surface. He was moving on a gurney or a cold hard table. One by one, bright white lights quickly passed above him. A smothering plastic device gripped the lower part of his face. He panicked, uttering a muffled squeal before someone cut a hole through the plastic, allowing air into his mouth.

Shadowy figures lurked above him. Their faces appeared differently, wide, oval eyes, gray complexions. They studied him as though he were a specimen, poking and prodding him, and then flashing a white light so bright into his eyes it sent a sharp pain through his head. They lowered a long tube down his throat as he squirmed and squealed. He felt a quick pumping and then slowly, they removed the tube, just as if they had pumped his stomach.

A long device lowered from above the table. It appeared as a suction device, throbbing and pulsating with a flowery motion. The device came down upon him, just between his legs. Brief feelings of ecstasy came and passed. He felt release, and then the suction device ascended upward and away.

The gray faces loomed over him, studying him, their heads bobbing from side to side in wonder. The next thing he knew, the bright white lights passed above him again. Then, he saw himself being gently lowered to the ground, the rocky expanse atop Eagle Rock Mountain. There, he slept, until he awoke and called Sidney.

But this was a dream, and in it, he didn't walk aimlessly waiting for Sidney to find him. This time, Dylan turned and saw the vast, grassy field he'd seen before in his dreams. He glimpsed the boy again, walking toward him from a distance. The boy wore the same hoodie jacket. His black bangs jutted out from beneath the hood. Soon, the boy stood before him, closer than before. He lowered the hood from his head. Dylan saw those eyes, those solid black orbs, no whites, no irises. He felt a chill as the boy stared through him. The boy pointed at him and in a warped, almost mechanical tone, cried out.

"Papa!"

Dylan jolted up from the bed, the sweat soaking his face and hair. Upon waking, he recalled Father Maguire's words to him.

"I'll be praying for you, Dylan, and that someday you remember."

Someday had just happened. This time, the dream progressed the whole way through. He remembered the series of events. He'd been abducted and experimented on. All of the memories of that night came flooding back to him. He hadn't seen a boy that night, but the boy appeared in his dream again, the mysterious boy who called him, "Papa." Who was he? Outside of the boy, everything finally became clear. Dylan remembered. He remembered everything.

Don't miss out on your next favorite book!

Join the Melange Books mailing list at
www.melange-books.com/mail.html

THANK YOU FOR READING

Did you enjoy this book?

We invite you to leave a review at the website of your choice, such as Goodreads, Amazon, Barnes & Noble, etc.

DID YOU KNOW THAT LEAVING A REVIEW...

- Helps other readers find books they may enjoy.
- Gives you a chance to let your voice be heard.
- Gives authors recognition for their hard work.
- Doesn't have to be long. A sentence or two about why you liked the book will do.

ABOUT THE AUTHOR

Christopher Carrolli is a full-time writer, who lives in Western Pennsylvania. He is a graduate of University of Pittsburgh at Greensburg and holds a BA in English Writing, and an AA in English. He has also won the Ida B. Wells Prize in Journalism.

www.christophercarrolli.blogspot.com
carrollic@aol.com

ALSO BY CHRISTOPHER CARROLLI

WITH MELANGE BOOKS

The Paranormal Investigator

Pipeline

The Listener

The Third Eye of Leah Leeds

The Skinwalker's Tale

Phantom in the Sky

Black Mirror

Shadows Among Us

Malevolent